Grave Markers
Volume 3

Dominic Stabile, Adrian Ludens,

and S.L. Williams

A
Grinning Skull Press
Publication

"Full Moon in the West" copyright ©2016 Dominic Stabile
    Originally published by Grinning Skull Press, December 22, 2016
"Bottled Spirits" copyright ©2016 Adrian Ludens
    Originally published by Grinning Skull Press, December 28, 2016
"The Dance" copyright ©2017 S.L. Williams
    Originally published by Grinning Skull Press, January 4, 2017

The Skull logo with stylized lettering was created for Grinning Skull Press by Dan Moran, http://dan-moran-art.com/.
Cover designed by Jeffrey Kosh, http://jeffreykosh.wix.com/jeffreykoshgraphics.

ISBN: 0-9986912-4-0
ISBN-13: 978-0-9986912-4-4

CONTENTS

A WORD ABOUT GRAVE MARKERS

I promise to keep this short so you can get on to reading the tales collected in this volume. Folks often ask about Grave Markers and what they are. Grave Markers are, in a word, novelettes. They are stories too long to be included in anthologies (which usually average 5,000 to 7,000 words) but not quite long enough to be published on their own as stand-alone novellas. They are published individually in digital formats, and then later compiled into a print collection. The reason why we started this line is we often heard authors commenting that there wasn't a market for those "in-between" length stories and we wanted to give them an outlet for such pieces. And that about sums it up. Told you I'd keep it short. Now, without further ado, I present to you the premier collection of Grave Markers. Enjoy!

Michael J. Evans
Grinning Skull Press

G S

GRAVE MARKER

Dominic Stabile

FULL MOON IN THE WEST

Chapter 1

Andréa Medina stopped the wagon in front of the sheriff's office. It was nearing evening, and the sun was a pink line on the horizon. Juan "Tezcat" Medina sat next to Andréa with his hands in his lap, his eyes on his soiled boots. He wore his father's tattered poncho and hat. The hat was too large for his head, and the poncho kept slipping from one shoulder. Andréa had made fun of him about it, saying he looked like a starved bandito. But the truth was he felt comforted by his father's clothing, and he was in great need of comfort.

Andréa moved to dismount, then turned to her brother. "We should speak with the sheriff, see if he has found anything."

"It is no use," Tezcat said.

Andrea slid back into her seat and gave her brother a hopeful look. "There is still time," she said.

"I cannot do it," Tezcat said. "Even if there is time, and the witch can do as she says, I cannot kill a man, much less six men."

"You can and you must."

3

"It is *my* wife and daughter," Tezcat said. "Why should I not let them lie in peace with God?"

Andrea's eyes widened, and she looked down at her feet a moment, considering his words. "Maria was my sister, Juana, my niece," she said, as if reaffirming her own convictions. "They are a part of me, as they are you. If you can bring them back, then that is what you must do."

Tezcat shook his head. "I should lust for revenge, but I do not." He looked at his sister. "You burn with it."

Andréa gripped his poncho and folded it back, revealing the Colt .45 on his hip. As they watched, the bullet chambers emitted a dim, purple glow that grew ever fainter, until it died.

"You brought the gun to Emygdia," she said. "Why did you accept her help if you do not want them back?"

"I do want them back," he said. "But not like this." He thought of the illusion the witch, Emygdia, had cast before the fire the night before: a dream-vision of his wife and daughter sleeping soundly, their skin glowing with life. *Bring me the souls of the six men who sent your wife and daughter across the river,* she had said, *and I will use them to bargain for your girls.*

Andréa shook her head and was about to argue further when a voice called out, "Help you two?"

Sheriff Watson stood leaning against the porch railing outside his office, smoking a cigarette. He was a white man, roughly six feet tall. He wore a full, white beard, and there was a cunning, amused quality to his expression, as if he were pulling off the greatest hoax of all time simply by standing where he was standing and wearing a star on his shirt.

"We have questions," Andréa said.

"Thought you might," Watson said, and he went back inside.

Andréa and Tezcat shared a wary glance, and then Andréa dismounted. After a moment spent watching the doorway through which Watson had just disappeared, Tezcat reluctantly followed.

Chapter 2

The Sheriff's desk was just to the left of the entrance, and behind that was a polished gun case containing a double-barrel shotgun, two Winchester repeaters, and several cartons of shells. Everything in the room, save the gun case, was covered in an even skin of dust and sand.

Sheriff Watson was standing in front of one of the two jail cells built into the back of the room, facing the man inside.

The Englishman.

Andréa and Tezcat stopped and stared at the man, unable to speak.

He was still wearing the black hat and expensive suit he'd worn the night he ordered the killing of Tezcat's wife and daughter, but some of the diamonds had left his smile. One of his blue eyes was swollen shut, and the other was as red as a bullet wound.

The Sheriff didn't turn. He stood there quietly smoking a moment, and then he said, "Caught up with him last night. I know a little about running from the Law myself, and this one's no good at it."

"I do not believe it," Andréa said.

"His friends were a sight better at fleeing, however," Watson said, ignoring her, "and I figured them to be in Mexico by now." He dropped his cigarette on the floor, stamped it out, and turned to face them. He was smiling. "But I worked our friend over anyways, just to be sure he couldn't put my mind at ease on that."

"What did he tell you?" Andréa said.

"It turns out they might have posted up somewhere nearby," Watson said, moving toward his desk and taking a seat. "Why are you so curious?"

"We are looking for them ourselves," Andréa said. "We went as far as Colina Verde, on the border, but no one has seen them."

"That so?" Watson said, smiling. He was looking at Tezcat.

"It is," Tezcat said. His voice shook, but his eyes were set firmly on the Englishman, who made a mocking sound somewhere between a laugh and a spat tooth.

"And what do you plan on doing when you find them?" Watson asked Andréa.

"What would you do?"

"I can tell you what I'll do if you and your brother decide to go vigilante," he said.

Andréa held his glare a moment, and then she turned to Tezcat. "Have you nothing to say?"

Tezcat was lost in the bloody eye of the Englishman, unconsciously playing his fingers over the butt of his pistol. He started at the mention of his name and saw that Watson and Andréa were watching him expectantly.

"I do not know if I can go through with it," he said.

The sheriff kept smiling. "What exactly are you up to?"

Tezcat had already turned back to the Englishman. He placed his hand on the butt of his gun again, trying to imagine pulling the trigger with a man on the other end of the barrel.

The sheriff observed this gesture and a gleam came into his eyes. "Heard you two rode out toward Barren Flats yesterday," he said. "You didn't happen to sit down with the witch now, did you?"

They looked at him without saying a word.

"Thought as much," Watson said, getting to his feet. "They're not God's problem yet," he said. "They got to pay my price first. They'll hang, then the good Lord can do what he pleases with them."

"We do not come with God," Andréa said.

The sheriff tensed for only a moment. "God. The Devil." He shrugged. "Makes no difference. This man and his raping, murdering friends will answer to the Law, and God and the Devil can watch." Watson sat back down and jerked his thumb toward the Englishman. "This one I'll keep close until his friends come for him, which they will."

"How do you know they will come for him?" Andréa asked.

"Turns out he's their leader."

Andréa looked at the Englishman and said, "What is a fop like you doing out here playing outlaw?"

"Playing?" the Englishman said. His calm voice was incongruous with his shattered face. "I'm not much for theatre. The fact is, I simply enjoy what I do." He nodded toward Tezcat. "Your wife, for example, was a toffer I won't soon forget. Do you know that, right before I cut her throat, she thanked me for the ride? I swear it's true."

Tezcat dropped to his knees. He had drawn his gun, but it fell from numb fingers and clattered to the floor. Andréa dropped to her knees and took her brother's face in her hands.

Watson got to his feet and marched toward the cell, taking a ring of keys from his pocket. He stood before the bars, and the Englishman rose, grinning at him. His teeth were the color of an old lemon peel.

"I warned you about running your mouth," Watson said, taking something from his pocket. At the sight of it, the Englishman scurried back to his cot. Watson opened the cell door and stood over the Englishman, who emitted a pathetic mewling sound similar to that of a wounded dog. And then Watson raised the object over his head and brought it down into the Englishman's face repeatedly until the prisoner stopped moving.

Watson backed out of the cell and locked the door. Then he went back to his desk and lit another cigarette.

Tezcat and Andréa stared at the mutilated prisoner. His face was swollen. A red gash crossed his forehead, and blood ran over his eyes. As they watched, he rose to a seated position on his cot. He drew a hand over his forehead and licked the blood from his fingers. He was in pain, but trying hard to appear as if he wasn't.

"The moon will heal my wounds," he said to Watson. "What about you, Sheriff?"

Watson took the cigarette from his mouth and exhaled smoke, as if he hadn't heard.

"The moon?" Tezcat said, feeling blood slowly flowing back into his face, his fingers. He looked at Watson. "What does he mean?" It was then he noticed the object the sheriff had used to bludgeon the prisoner. Andréa rose to her feet when she saw it as well.

A large, silver crucifix, covered in blood.

"Borrowed that from Father Lucas," Watson said. He stood, walked around his desk, and went to the window, looking out at the street.

"Like I said, I worked him over," Watson said, "and he had a story to tell. More than I wanted to hear, that's for sure. But enough so I know what I'm dealing with."

"And what is that?" Andréa said.

Watson glanced at them, and an uncharacteristic look of bashfulness crossed his face before he turned his eyes back out the window. "Skinwalkers," he said.

Chapter 3

Andréa laughed out loud. "They are bad men, and they are monsters. But they are not *MONsters*," she said.

Watson kept his eyes on the street. "They are, girl. And it makes a whole helluva lot of sense, too."

"What sense does it make?" Tezcat asked.

Watson exhaled a long breath. "You know how Doc Greely has his place out to the west of town?"

"Yes, so?" Andréa said.

"He's within spitting distance of those caves out by Briar Cliff Gorge. And he came to me one morning about a month ago looking like a man who hadn't slept a night in his life. His eyes all bloodshot, his hands shaking with sleeplessness. What was more, he was embarrassed. It took me a second to pick up on it, but once I had, I couldn't believe it. Old hard-ass Doc Greely was tip-toeing up my porch steps, hat in his hands like a boy who'd shat his pants. And when he finally spit out the words he wanted to say, I laughed. I thought he'd taken too many of his own horse-piss-and-water snake oil concoctions.

"'I've been hearing howling in the caves off my property,' he said. And when I suggested it was wolves or coyotes, he said, 'These howls did not come from anything of this world.'

"Just like that. That's when I laughed. But he just looked at me, earnest. You can tell when a man like Greely is joking because he has no aptitude for it. And you can tell when a man like Greely is telling the truth because he's not joking, and men like Greely only speak of the uncanny when they're stumbling over a bad joke or when they mean it."

Watson looked at Andréa, and then Tezcat. "And he meant it."

"You're saying this man and the men who killed my wife and daughter are Skinwalkers?" Tezcat said. His tone held the shocked disbelief he thought it should hold, but he almost believed it, looking at the prisoner, who grinned big behind those iron bars.

Watson nodded.

"How do you know?" Andréa said, pointing at the prisoner. "Because that madman said so?"

"Because I heard the howls myself," he said. "Because I tracked our friend here out to those caves last night, and caught up to him before he could slink down into the dark. I saw the tracks out there in the sand outside those caves, and I know plenty about the Indian legends regarding such creatures. I heard the howls on my way back. It was dark, and that sunset everyone's so crazy about looked like blood pooled up on the horizon. I heard the howls echoing from those caves, so loud and sharp I thought they were coming up behind me.

The sound of it." He paused. Eyes narrowed, he stared out the window, his mouth working as he relived the memory. "Like men being torn apart."

Tezcat and Andréa stood silently.

Watson looked at them again. "They'll come tonight."

"How do you know?" Tezcat asked.

"Tonight starts the full moon," Watson said. "They're strongest during the full moon."

And that's when the gunshot sounded, and a bullet ripped through the window and hit Watson in the shoulder. He spun to the right and fell across his desk, sliding to the floor in a heap. Dust rose up from the floor in a cloud, and Watson gripped his shoulder and shut his eyes against the dust. He coughed, rolled, and got to his feet. He drew the .44 from his hip holster and blindly fired two rounds out the window.

Tezcat and Andréa had dropped to the floor. They stayed there a moment. Watson fell onto his backside and listened, his breath coming in heaves.

There was no return fire.

Tezcat stood up just enough to look out the window. He saw one of the Englishman's posse out there, riding back and forth on a horse, his gun drawn. Long, greasy black hair hung from a worn bucket hat. He wore a sheen of dust from his shredded duster to his mud-caked boots. Though Tezcat couldn't see his face, he knew the man had a scar that cut a pink river through his beard, from eye to jawbone. This was the man who had killed Juana.

"Send him out, Sheriff!" the man called, his horse bucking and moving in fevered circles, as if it wanted to get rid of its rider and make a break for Mexico. "Save your town a whole lotta grief."

"Not gonna happen," Watson called back.

Three more shots followed, two of which came through the window on Tezcat's side of the room, and he hit the floor just as shards of glass rained over him. The third bullet pierced the door and skittered across the floor into the empty jail cell.

"That was your one warning, Sheriff," the rider called out. "You made my day. Me and the boys are gonna love tearin' you and your friends apart. We'll be watching outside town. You try to move him, we'll know. You try to run, we'll know."

"I'm pissing," Watson yelled back, but Tezcat saw the fear in his eyes.

"It's the full moon tonight, Sheriff," the rider shouted. "I can feel it already. You're gonna die, Sheriff. Slow. Slower than those two Mexican bitches we took the other day. You'll see, Sheriff."

Tezcat stood and moved toward the window in a red haze of fury. He drew his gun and fired at the man on the horse. The gun howled, and a funnel of flame blazed from the barrel, but the man had already spurred his mount and was gunning it for the west end of town. A moment passed; Tezcat's blood cooled, and he was filled back up with the sense of emptiness he had lived under since the day he lost his family. He slid to his knees and fell against the wall, his heart pounding. He looked out the way the rider had gone, and he could see stone-colored clouds moving toward town, and in the distance, rough winds had swept up a fog of sand that obscured the horizon. And kneeling there staring out at that dark, whirling wall closing in, he thought he might be ready to kill a man after all. At least these few.

He got to his feet, turned to face the room, and saw that Watson, Andréa, and the Englishman were staring at him, eyes wide. After a moment of confused silence, he realized what they were looking at: the chambers of his pistol were emitting that purple glow again, but this time the light was so full and bright, the shape of the gun was almost completely obscured; it appeared as though he was holding a ball of purple fire. The barrel was glowing orange-hot, as if he'd stuck it into a blacksmith's forge.

Chapter 4

The Sheriff's deputy, Jack Russell, came in after the rider had left, and he got Doc Greely, and Greely patched up the Sheriff's shoulder.

"Not so bad," Deputy Russell said after the doctor left. He was sitting on the edge of Watson's desk. His eyes hung lax in a confident way, and his voice rolled soft and even, like he was thinking aloud.

Watson had taken a bottle of whiskey from his desk, and he was working his way through it. "Get off my desk, and don't act like you got iron balls all a sudden."

Russell stood up quick, but he kept the confident look. "How we gonna do this, Sheriff?"

"I want you to get out there and make sure people are off the street. When they come, they ain't going to waste time. They're coming right for us. So long as people stay indoors and the doors are barred, they're liable to be fine."

"You think that's true, Sheriff?" Russell said.

"Shit if I know," Watson said. "Just do it, and get back here quick as you can."

Russell left.

Watson's eyes immediately settled on Tezcat, who sat next to Andréa on a wooden bench against the far wall. Watson took another long drink from the bottle, then said, "That was some magic trick."

"The witch," Tezcat managed before Andréa elbowed him.

"Let him talk," Watson said.

Andréa and Tezcat looked down at their laps.

"Listen," Watson said. "We're stuck here together. Whatever plans you came here with, you got to toss them. We're wolf shit, we don't work together."

The Englishman laughed. "A lamb with the will to fight is still just a lamb," he said.

"These lambs got guns," Watson said.

"Guns don't kill us, Sheriff," the Englishman said.

"No?" Watson nodded toward Tezcat. "Something tells me that one might. What you say, Tez?"

Tezcat glanced at Andréa and then turned back to Watson.

"We did go to the witch last night," he said.

"I already know that," Watson said. He pointed toward Tezcat's pistol. "Ain't that your daddy's old gun?"

"I have always kept it," Tezcat said, nervously clicking the cylinder from one chamber to the next, "but have never used it. My father used it for no more than shooting bottles and the occasional coyote. It has not worked since I was a child."

"Works fine now," Watson said.

"The witch took it, and she whispered some words, and now it shoots. And she said, when I shoot one of the six men who took my wife and daughter, his soul will fill the empty chamber." He glanced up at Watson to read his expression. Watson looked like he was in pain and starting to get drunk. "When I have all six souls, I must return the gun to her, and she will use the six souls to barter for the souls of my wife and daughter."

"Barter?" Watson said.

"I told you to stay quiet," Andréa said. "He will never understand, and you will look like a fool."

"Give me some credit," Watson said. "I'm the one who believes in monsters, remember?"

Andréa didn't say anything.

"Dawn," Tezcat said, his eyes on the gun. "I have until dawn. After that, Maria and Juana — their souls will be beyond Emygdia's reach, and they will be lost forever."

Watson had managed to light another cigarette, and he watched Tezcat a moment, smoking and taking long pulls from the bottle. "Why all six?" he asked.

Tezcat shrugged. "She says she knows these men. She gave them a gift, and they have abused it. She said I have to bring all six souls. Two of them to trade for Maria and Juana. The other four, I do not know. It is her price."

Watson turned to the Englishman. "What gift?"

The Englishman smiled. "I overestimated you, Sheriff," he said. "I was sure you would have worked that out yourself."

Everyone sat quietly for a moment.

"The moon?" Tezcat said, glaring at the Englishman. "Emygdia gave you the power to change?"

The Englishman leaped to his feet and held out his hands toward Tezcat, as if he were presenting the sheriff with a prize pony. "And here we have a man of intelligence!"

Tezcat looked at Andréa. "Emygdia helped these men become monsters?" he said, his voice rising in anger. "You say she is good, that she looks out for the good of the people here. How can that be, knowing this?"

"I did not know," Andréa said. "I still do not know that what the sheriff says is true. That these men are Skinwalkers."

"Patience, Meat," the Englishman said. "You will know soon enough."

"Keep your mouth shut," Watson said, "and maybe I won't let Tez blast you off this earth right now."

The Englishman tried to look unmoved, but his eyes fell on Tezcat's gun, and he closed his mouth.

"We should kill him now," Andréa said. "One less to worry about."

"Nothing would make me happier," Watson said, "but that's not how the Law works."

"The Law?" Andréa said. "Do you think that costume makes you a lawman?"

"I think the badge does," Watson said. "Whoever I might have been before I came here, I'm Sheriff now, and no vigilante's gonna walk into my office and plug one of my prisoners. I like you kids. Always have. Your momma and daddy were my friends. But let's get this straight: you go for my prisoner, I'll put you down."

"And what of the men coming to free him?" Andréa said.

"You won't be here for that," Watson said. He looked at Tezcat. "You leave your daddy's gun here with me and head over to the church. There's a basement in there where you should be safe. There's only one entrance, and it's a heavy door. Not to mention that's hallowed ground, and I figure that might count for something. If I happen to collect any souls, I'll make sure you get 'em before dawn."

"What happened to us working together?" Andréa said.

"That was before I knew all the power was in that gun," Watson said. "That being the case, I don't reckon it matters who's holding it."

"You cannot defeat them alone," Tezcat said.

"I got Russell," Watson said, taking another pull from the bottle. "We've made do in worse situations."

"I find it hard to believe you have been in a worse situation," Andréa said.

"Oh, it's hard to believe," Watson said, and he turned his red face toward the ceiling, thinking a moment. When he began to speak, his voice held the hushed tone of a confession.

Chapter 5

"Russell and me were on the run together before we came here," he said. "He was just a boy then, and I was a young man. We had Pinkerton after us, of all the lawmen there could have been, after a poorly planned train robbery. Three of our boys got nabbed, and one was killed. But me and Russell got away, made our slow way down to Mexico. At night we'd make camp in the unappealing places you wouldn't normally think to. And when you're out in the desert at night, freezin' your ass off with no fire because you're too scared to make one, you see the sorts of things that come out when they think no one's around. Just shapes was what we saw. Black, ugly shapes set against the deep gray of the sky."

He paused a moment, raised the bottle to drink, then decided against it and set the bottle back down on the desk. "There was this one night, we were a day away from the border and our freedom. We'd made camp in a cactus-filled trench between a crag and a series of boulders. We'd wedged ourselves between the cacti and wrapped ourselves up in blankets, and I was about out when I heard this noise. A howl, just like those howls I heard coming from the caves to the west of town last night. But this was close. So close, the pure volume of it had me clenching my teeth. Russell was just a boy, like I said, and if I was a little scared, he was shitting holes in his pants.

"Russell started fidgeting, and he was calling my name out, quietly at first, and then louder, panicking. I couldn't rightly get to him through the patch of cacti, and I knew better than to start shouting back to him. So I found a little rock and flung it at his head; it hit home, and when he turned and looked at me, I saw the relief on his face. But then a shadow fell over our little trench, and his face changed, and I knew then something was standing over me.

"I went still. But Russell, again, was a boy, and a dumb one if anyone's asking. He gets to his knees, cactus prongs sticking into his hands and wrists, as he's just grabbing for anything to get him to his feet so he can run. Well, I guess the thing didn't see me, and I hadn't seen it yet, because I was still. But I saw it a second later. Something like a coyote, but on two legs, tattered shreds of a fed's uniform hanging from its thin body. A shiny silver star was still pinned to what was left of its shirt. That body was covered in a thick, almost gorgeous pelt, but you could see places where the skin had torn during its change. Strips of muscle and tendon gleamed in the moonlight, and there was a smell — a barn smell, I guess. This thing stepped right over me, either figuring I was so still I must be dead or that I was bigger and slower and he could catch up to me later, I don't know. But its yellow eyes were on the boy.

"I didn't know much about Skinwalkers at the time, so I reached down into my blanket to pull my .44. Russell was tangled up in his blanket and the cacti, and he was so scared he couldn't even shout. I was delirious with the madness of it all, but my head was just clear enough to figure we were both dead no matter what I did. Pulling my gun was as natural and as futile as a rooster puffing its chest at a rattle-snake. But I pulled it, and I'd trained it on the thing's hunched back when a gunshot sounded from somewhere behind me, and the creature let out a cry I'll never forget. It was like you took a man's pipes and wired 'em up with a coyote's and then pumped air through them. It was a horrible, sad, tormented sound; like Hell's door had swung open on Torture Tuesday.

"It ran off, and the boy had fainted, and I lay back down, wedging myself into the cacti, not knowing if the thing might come back or who the men were that had fired the shot. The thing never came back, but the men who were after it passed right over us. Men in long, black coats or robes, I couldn't tell. Long beards and hair, and weapons hanging from them that looked to be made of silver. Large crosses hung from chains around their necks. They passed right by, like I said, speaking a language I've never heard again to this day. They didn't see us, and we didn't wait until morning to move on. I was up, and I slapped Russell until he got up, and we made Mexico by the following afternoon."

Chapter 6

Everyone was quiet as Watson dabbed out his cigarette, half smoked, and lit another one. He smoked for a while, and then glanced toward the Englishman. "Maybe a friend of yours."

"I doubt I was even alive at a point in time when you could have reasonably been referred to as a 'young man'," the Englishman said.

Watson gave a small grunt of a laugh. "An age joke. I find that beneath you, *old boy*."

"Apologies," the Englishman said. He wiped blood from his eyes. "It appears I'm not at my best at the moment."

"If you are both finished," Andréa said. "Sheriff, you need us. Even by the story you just told, you and Deputy Russell would have died if not for the intervention of others."

"Yeah, I guess. Now that I think of it, we got lucky. But that don't change the two most important things you need to know: one, that you two ain't deputized, and two, if I'm not mistaken, neither of you can shoot for shit."

"We shoot well enough," Andréa said. "Deputize us."

"Why does she not allow the widower to speak?" the English-man said.

Andréa stared at the prisoner. He was grinning, and it appeared as if the wound on his forehead had begun to heal. He sat with his hands folded in his lap, awaiting her reply. But she glanced at Tezcat and then down at her lap.

"What do you say, Tez?" Watson said. "This is *your* revenge tale, ain't it? Why don't you decide what you're gonna do, so long as you know the only right answer is to give me your gun and hoof it over to the church."

Tezcat looked at the Englishman for a moment, and he thought of what the rider outside had said about his wife and daughter. He thought about the night it all happened. Today had been the longest he'd been without a drink since that night, and he'd been forced to remember the cries of Juana and Maria, the way the Englishman and his posse had laughed at their pleas for mercy. The memory of their cries became so clear in his mind at times that he would jump, as if startled by the sound.

"I do not know if I can kill a man," Tezcat said. He looked at Watson. "But I know that I must try. I believe the witch tells the truth, that she can do as she says. I cannot leave it in your hands, Sheriff. Could you?"

"No," Watson said, with barely a moment's hesitation. "No, I couldn't do that. But I've got the benefit of outside perspective. You're nose-down in rage and sorrow. I'm clear-headed. And from where I sit, this ain't about you getting your revenge or raising the dead. This is about me getting justice for our little town."

"You won't help us?" Andréa said.

Watson took another pull from the bottle. "I don't much care for magic. And the way I see it, magic is what got us all into this mess. No, I won't help you help the witch. If I have my way, these boys will look into my eyes just before they die, knowing a man with a star on his shirt put them down. That the Law won." He looked at Tezcat. "Your wife and daughter were two of the sweetest ladies this world ever saw. And if there's a heaven, I got no doubt that's where they are right now. Why not leave them to eternal peace, Tez?"

"I know that I should," Tezcat said. "But I cannot."

Just then, the front door burst open and Deputy Russell rushed in. He'd lost his confident look, traded it for a wide-eyed alertness, and his voice trembled with adrenaline and fear as he said, "They're coming."

Chapter 7

Sheriff Watson unlocked the gun case. He took out the two repeaters and the double barrel and dropped them on the desk along with the boxes of shells. As he and Deputy Russell loaded the guns, he said, "Y'all two should have listened to me. Looks like you're in it now."

"In all honesty, we could use the help, Sheriff," Russell said.

"Don't contradict me," Watson said. "Just load the shotgun and give it to Tez. Tez, hand your daddy's gun over. I'll be using it."

"No," Tezcat said.

"We ain't got time," Watson said.

Russell finished loading the shotgun and held it out to Tezcat.

Tezcat placed his hand on the butt of his gun and took a step back. "I have my gun," he said. He looked at Watson. "I must do this myself."

"Are you going to take such disrespect from this little *pocho*?" the Englishman said.

"Shut your goddamned mouth," Watson said. "Tez, I'm not

askin' —"

The sheriff was interrupted by a piercing howl, distant, but distinct in its ring of agony.

They all stopped and listened, eyes wide, muscles tense with expectation. Tezcat went to the window and looked out. Those gray clouds were directly over the town, and a heavy rain had begun to pour, quickly turning the streets into a swamp. And he could see the shadowed figures riding in from the west of town, as the beat of their horses' hooves shook the floor and grew into a heavy, rising thrum he first took for thunder. He noticed something off about the figures on the horses. The shadows he saw were not the shadows of men, but something between man and beast. They rode crouched, and their limbs swung out to their sides at times, and he understood that they were in mid-change.

As he backed away from the window, a hand fell on his shoulder and spun him around. Watson stood over him, glaring down at him. His face was grim, and beads of sweat clung to his beard. After a tense moment, Watson took Tezcat's hand and slapped a box of .45 caliber shells into it.

"Reload," Watson said.

Tezcat nodded and began to reload his father's gun.

The sheriff went to the window with one of the rifles and broke out the glass and took a knee. Deputy Russell went to the window on the other side of the door and did the same. The smell of rain entered the room.

"They're comin' up," Russell said.

"I see them," Watson said. He glanced over his shoulder. "Andréa, man the shotgun. Any of these bastards get past us and come through the door, make sure they don't feel welcome. Tez, goddammit, this ain't about you or your revenge, but you can keep your daddy's gun. Regular guns ain't likely to do shit but slow them down, so we'll be counting on you to put the final bullet in them. I left my keys on the desk. Things don't go our way, you and your sis lock yourselves in the other cell. These bastards are tough and mean, but they ain't gonna chew through iron."

The Englishman laughed at this as if he were enjoying the futility of their movements.

Andréa took the shotgun from the sheriff's desk, broke it open, and checked to make sure it was loaded. Then she snapped it shut, crouched behind one end of the sheriff's desk, and watched the door. Tezcat drew his father's gun, crouched behind the sheriff, and looked out the window. Five horses passed by, putting deep tracks in the mud — but there were no riders.

"You see 'em?" Russel said.

"Nope," Watson said.

"They changed," Tezcat said.

The sheriff stood, but kept his gun aimed out toward the street, where a few of the horses lingered, padding in circles. "I know."

Just then the rain picked up; a flash of lightening lit up the street and a blast of thunder shook shreds of glass from the windowsill.

Tezcat saw shapes moving low to the ground. They were so quick and vague, he wasn't sure if his eyes were merely playing tricks or not. The shapes would blend with the shadows of the horses a moment, and then a moment later they would appear again, closer. The noise of wind and rain made it so Tezcat could not hear them, but he knew they were coming. He stepped back from the window and raised his gun over the sheriff's head, readying himself.

"You okay, Tez?" the sheriff whispered.

"I am," Tezcat said.

"Good," the sheriff said, "because we're gonna need you."

Deputy Russell fired first. There was the bright flash of fire from his rifle, and in that brief light, Tezcat saw that two of the things had reached the porch. One was crouched just on the other side of his window, its head nearly touching the sheriff's rifle, and the other was on Russell's side.

Tezcat stepped back instinctively and tripped, falling straight onto his backside. At the same time, the sheriff jumped to his feet and fired a poorly aimed shot out into the road. He cocked his gun and fired from the hip repeatedly, backing away from the window as he did so. The one that had been crouching outside pulled itself into the window with two large, clawed hands. Long fingers shimmered with a gleam of smoke-colored fur. Its face was concealed by the dark beyond the window, but light from the room glinted off its eyes and teeth.

"Christ in a manger," Watson said, stopping to reload.

Tezcat got to his feet and fired two shots out the window, missing both times. The creature had moved so quickly he had thought it was still there.

Deputy Russell was still firing, and the one that had been outside his window now retreated back down the steps. As Tezcat approached the window again, he could see the shadows of the beasts moving out on the road.

It was then the howl came from the cell behind them. They all turned and saw that the Englishman had changed. He still wore his long coat, though it was torn at the shoulders, and his hat sat cocked on his head. His pelt was pitch black, and his eyes glowed the same purple that came from Tezcat's gun. His long snout was open slightly in a grin.

Tezcat raised his gun toward The Englishman and took a deep breath as he called to mind the image Emygdia had shown him of his wife and daughter, alive again. Just as he pulled the trigger, Sheriff Watson brought the barrel of his rifle down on Tezcat's arm, and the pistol fired a bullet uselessly into the floorboards. Tezcat dropped to his knees, gripping his forearm. The gun slipped from his hand and clattered to the floor.

"What are you doing?" Tezcat cried.

"That's *my* prisoner," Watson said.

Then, suddenly, Russell fired another shot, but this one blew one of the legs right off the sheriff's desk. The desk toppled to one side, casting loose rifle shells onto the floor.

"What the hell was that?" Watson said, turning toward his deputy.

Deputy Russell stood before his window, facing them. He had one hand clasped to his throat, while the trigger finger of his other hand pulled uselessly on the trigger of his rifle. Blood shot in jets from between the fingers over his throat, and he made the raspy, panting sound a dog makes when it's overheated.

Watson made to run toward his deputy, but the door burst from its hinges and struck the sheriff on his left side, sending him across the room. Cold rain rushed through the door on a gust of wind, and behind that came one of the Englishman's posse. He moved on all fours until he cleared the doorway, then he stood up straight. He looked much like the creature the sheriff had described in his story, except instead of a torn shirt with a silver star on it, this one wore most of a long leather duster, leather boots, and a gun belt. Its jaw moved as it chewed something. Blood ran from its long snout, dripped from the long white whiskers hanging from its chin. Its eyes weren't yellow, but purely and horribly human. They were brown, and there was a touch of amusement in them, as if the man inside were watching and enjoying himself.

Tezcat noticed the pink scar running down its face from eye to jawbone. He took his father's gun from the floor and dropped the hammer, but the creature swept its clawed hand back and knocked it from his grasp. The gun landed on a corner table next to one of the windows. The creature, acting on instinct, grabbed for the gun on its belt, but its fingers and claws were too long. After a moment, it gave up and lunged for Tezcat, claws bared.

There was a deafening report, and the creature changed course in mid-air and slammed into the table on which Tezcat's gun sat. Tezcat turned to see Andréa breaking open the shotgun and removing the empty shells and loading two more. "Get the gun!" she cried, as she snapped the shotgun shut. She raised the gun toward the open doorway as another beast poked its hideous head in, and she gave it both barrels. There was a deafening shriek, and it disappeared from the doorway. Andréa reloaded, and then dropped to the floor next to Deputy Russell, who had stopped making that panting noise. He was looking up at the ceiling, his mouth moving as if he were thinking of a song he really liked.

Tezcat started for his gun, but the creature with the scar blocked him, and as he moved, it stirred and got to its feet. Tezcat turned, looking for help, and saw that Sheriff Watson had fallen against The Englishman's cell. The Englishman had five claws in the sheriff's chest and a jaw full of teeth in the sheriff's right shoulder.

Andréa got to her feet and ran toward the cell, pressing the shotgun against The Englishman's head and pulling the trigger. There was another report. The Englishman's hat flew off, and there was a meaty, wet hole where one of his ears had been. He let go of the sheriff, but no sooner had the sheriff hit the floor and rolled away, then the Englishman was at the bars again, clawing at him, his beastly face a matted mess of bloody fur.

The sheriff took up his rifle in one hand and fired a shot toward the creature with the scar. The shot missed, but it distracted the creature long enough for Tezcat to cross the room and take up Deputy Russell's rifle. He turned and fired as the creature lunged at him. The bullet blew its lower jaw clean off, but it didn't go down. Tezcat cocked the rifle and put another bullet through its eye. A gum, like melted taffy, boiled from the empty socket. This time it dropped down to all fours and smashed into a wall trying to get out the door.

Tezcat went for his father's gun, but another of the creatures leaped through the window on that side of the room, its broad shoulders breaking through the windowsill. Shreds of splintered wood and broken glass scattered across the floor, and it stood between him and the gun. It had to be seven and a half feet tall. By some miracle, a white Stetson sat on its head, unmolested by the change or the window. Tezcat cocked the rifle and fired. He did this three more times. The creature, unfazed, swung its massive claw at Tezcat, who dropped to the floor and rolled toward the deputy. Deputy Russell now stared motionlessly at the ceiling, his eyes open and stripped of sight.

Andréa's shotgun exploded over Tezcat's head, and the creature stumbled back a step, then started toward Tezcat again.

Tezcat rose to his knees, cocked the rifle, and pulled the trigger, but the gun only clicked.

The creature swung another claw at Tezcat's head. He ducked under it, took the rifle by the barrel, and swung it at the creature. The wooden stock cracked over its ankle, and it cried out and dropped to the floor. Andréa unloaded two more shells into its bloodied pelt. Sheriff Watson had moved back to the window, and he was firing out at the other beasts trying to enter the room.

Gunfire and smoke filled the air, making it difficult to breathe or focus. The horrible cries of the beasts cut through the chaos like the shriek of wind through a violent storm. Tezcat desperately vaulted the downed creature's slumped body as the one with the scar came back through the door, the vague light of the room catching the glint of its mutilated eye. Sheriff Watson raised his rifle to its head and pulled the trigger. The gun clicked, and the beast thrust its hand into Watson's belly and wrenched it back out with a grunt. A worm of intestine came with it, and the creature's hand dripped with thick blood. Watson dropped to his knees.

Tezcat picked up his father's gun, turned, and fired a round into the bloodied face of the beast with the scar. The bullet entered through the creature's mouth, and a shadow of blood and brains flew off into the night like a bat.

The fight stopped suddenly. Everyone watched Tezcat as a beam of purple light stretched from the barrel of his gun to the corpse of the creature he'd just shot. The gun was again a bright purple ball in his hand, only this time he felt an immense heat. His heart raced, and he was full of what he thought must be the kind of divine joy they talked about in the Bible. A holy joy. There was a sharp crackle, like static electricity. And then the creature's corpse exploded in a red mist.

They all stood there a moment. Even the wolf with the Stetson watched, as if in reverence for the very power that allowed it to exist. Then it turned on Tezcat and clawed for the gun. Tezcat took a step back and fired. The bullet made a little round hole just below the creature's ribcage, and a flap of its back skin swung around to the front like a shutter blown open by the wind. Its hands stretched out for Tezcat even as its feet left the floor, and it appeared, for a moment, as if it were swimming through the air. It hit the floor, and there was the purple beam of light. The light glinted off the eyes of the creatures watching from the doorway and through the broken windows. And then the creature with the Stetson exploded into a cloud of red mist, just like the other one. The Stetson sat unsoiled in the pool of blood and fur that remained.

Tezcat was elated. He'd never felt this before. All apprehension he'd felt over the idea of taking a life had left him. Now he *wanted* to kill. He wanted to kill them all, and then do it over again.

He aimed the pistol, glowing with a purple fire, the barrel bright orange like a burning coal, toward the vague figures beyond the door and fired repeatedly. But the hammer of the pistol was clicking against empty chambers before he realized the shadows had moved. He wondered if they had been there at all.

"Quickly, Tezcat!" Andréa cried. She had opened the door to the empty cell and was waving Tezcat in.

He turned back toward the bench against the wall, where he'd left the case of bullets the sheriff had handed him, but one of the beasts was pulling itself through the busted window on that side of the room. This one wore a pair of golden pistols on its hips.

Tezcat bolted across the room and dropped to his knees next to the bench. He tipped the box of shells onto the bench and grabbed a handful. The beast with the golden pistols came through the window and rushed him.

Andréa's shotgun thundered from the cell, and the shot tore off a hunk of the creature's left shoulder. It dropped down to all fours, but it kept coming.

Tezcat managed to get one round into the cylinder. He snapped it shut, dropped onto his back, and fired as the beast leaped at him. The bullet struck its throat, and its head floated up toward the ceiling with a tail of blood and sinew behind it as the body continued to gallop awkwardly for two more steps before falling over Tezcat like a desperate lover.

Andréa helped Tezcat out from beneath the body before it, too, exploded into the atmosphere.

Tezcat wheeled on the front door, his empty gun raised. Andréa broke open her shotgun, loaded two more shells and popped it shut.

They watched the entrance a moment, both of them covered in blood, their breaths coming in violent heaves — and something slowly dawned on them.

It was quiet.

The horses had left the street, and the rain had calmed to a drizzle.

"There are two more," Tezcat said.

"Where are they?" Andréa said.

Tezcat shook his head, but was too frightened to answer. He slowly reached into his pocket and removed the bullets he'd taken from the bench. He began to reload and noticed that three of the chambers were blocked by bullet-shaped stones. Looking closer, he saw that light permeated the stones, but only just.

"Their souls," Andréa said, looking over his shoulder. "As black as their deeds."

Tezcat loaded the remaining chambers and cocked back the hammer. It was only then he noticed how quiet The Englishman's cell had become. He turned back to see the cell empty, a hole ripped into the floor.

A chorus of howls wailed in the street. Tezcat hurried to the window and looked out. The horses were gone. Three shapes stood out there. He squinted his eyes. They were huddled close, passing something between them.

"What are they doing?" Andréa said. She had come up behind him and was looking over his shoulder.

He leaned on the broken windowsill, peering out for a better look. "I do not know," he said.

Then there was a loud report, a flame flashed at the center of the three figures outside, and a hunk of the windowsill shattered into a thousand shreds of splintered wood. The sawdust got in Tezcat's eyes, and he wiped it away and pulled Andréa to the floor.

"They are shooting?" Andréa said.

There were three shots in quick succession. More wood chips flew. A bullet sparked against one of the bars of the jail cells.

"They are shooting," Tezcat said.

More shots rang out into the night. All three of the beasts were firing now.

Tezcat tried to take position in the window to get a shot off, but a bullet buzzed past his head and his father's hat fell to the floor. He dropped backed down as two more rounds struck the windowsill.

"Great," Andréa said over the noise of the barrage. "Not only can they eat us, but they can shoot, too?"

"They cannot reload," Tezcat said.

Andréa faced the doorway, and her eyes widened. "They might not need to," she said, and raised the shotgun toward the doorway and fired. Tezcat rolled over and saw the beast that had been creeping up on them through the doorway. It stumbled back with a web of pellet holes across its chest. A .44, much like the sheriff's, flew from its malformed claws.

Tezcat took aim with his father's gun, preparing to finish it off, but a hairy arm reached in through the window above him. Long, black claws raked over his left thigh, slicing through fabric and flesh. He cried out and tried to jerk his leg back, but the creature's claws were embedded in the muscle. He was hooked. Andréa stood and trained the shotgun on the creature's arm.

There was another report from outside. Andréa's right breast opened up, and the blood that flowed out looked, for the moment, like a cut of fine, red fabric unfolding from her chest before it splattered to the floor. She dropped to her knees and looked directly into Tezcat's eyes.

"I love you, *Hermano*," she said. And then she fell forward. Dust rose up from the floor in a cloud about her.

Tezcat stared at her prone body and felt his heart turn cold. It surprised him that the expression could be taken literally. His heart was, in fact, cold. It was so cold it burned. But he no longer felt the pain in his leg, or the pain of loss, or the fear of God. He felt rage in its purest form. And he felt, finally, the need for righteous vengeance that he had tried so hard to summon since the night his wife and daughter had been taken.

The beast Andréa had shot was moving back through the doorway. Tezcat's gun bucked, and a wide hole formed in the creature's chest. It flew back against the porch railing. The railing gave way, and the beast stumbled out into the road. The purple beam of light trailed from the barrel of Tezcat's pistol to the creature's body even as he turned the weapon toward the hairy arm reaching through the window. The creature had leaned its upper body into the room, and it stretched its long, narrow muzzle toward Tezcat's leg.

Tezcat's gun roared, and the creature's snout exploded in a cloud of blood, bone, and teeth. It cocked its head back reflexively, its purple tongue hanging from the ruined mess of its face, and struck the top of the windowsill. It fell forward again. Tezcat got to his knees, rammed the barrel of his gun into the creature's face, and fired. The windowsill turned red, and a moment later the beast's body exploded into a mist so fine it never settled, but flew out toward the road and up, above where the Englishman stood with his six gun raised.

Tezcat stood in the doorway, favoring one leg, and fired a shot toward the shape of the Englishman, but the Englishman moved so quickly Tezcat thought he must have fired at a shadow by mistake. The Englishman's gun flashed, and Tezcat felt an impact in his left side, just below the ribcage. He fell to one knee. Heat filled the area of his bullet wound. He focused on breathing a moment. Then he took a bullet from his pocket and loaded it into the last empty chamber of his pistol. The other five chambers carried the five dark souls of the beasts he'd killed. He tried to lift the gun toward the final beast, the Englishman, but the Englishman wasn't there.

Then the creature was right in front of him. A strong, hairy hand clasped his throat and lifted him out of the light of the sheriff's office into the darkness of the night. He was carried out toward the center of the street. He could smell the creature. The barn smell Watson had spoken of. The creature grunted as it walked, and there was an impatient speed to its gait, as if it had somewhere else to be and killing Tezcat was a minor duty it would fulfill as mechanically as a blacksmith hammered iron. The sky was a clear, ash-colored slate stretched over them, as if God had closed the world's lid, knowing how this story ended. The moon was fat and round, and Tezcat thought he'd likely never seen such a beautiful moon. His shirt was wet with blood. The shirt stuck to his skin, and the blood quickly cooled in the night air.

When they reached the center of the street, the beast held its face close to Tezcat's. The Englishman's blue eyes stared out at him from the distorted face. Its breath was hot and smelled of blood and sulfur. For a time, it simply stared at him, and Tezcat kept expecting it to open its mouth and latch its jaws over his face.

Tezcat's arms hung limply at his sides. He was hypnotized by the pain of his wounds, and the crushing knowledge that his revenge would go unclaimed. The beast opened its mouth, as Tezcat had been imagining. Only the mouth opened much wider than he'd thought it could, and the Englishman moved slowly, savoring the moment. Tezcat numbly watched the maw of death close in. Then he felt the weight of the pistol he still held in his hand, and with a last push of exertion, he raised the pistol, pressed the barrel against the creature's heart, and pulled the trigger. The gun barked. A spray of the creature's blood showered the dirt with a light patter, like a sudden and brief burst of rain.

The Englishman's hand loosened on Tezcat's throat. Tezcat hit the dirt and fell straight back. He lay there and stared up at the creature. It fell to one side, and a moment later it was mist. Tezcat watched the light, red cloud of it float away on the night breeze.

Chapter 8

Tezcat limped back inside the sheriff's office holding the wound in his side. It wasn't as bad as he'd first thought, though he wished it had killed him. The sheriff had died on his knees in the doorway, propped up by his rifle. Andréa lay face down on the floor where she'd fallen. He stood in the doorway, looking down at her for a time.

"I love you, *Hermana*," he said.

Then he took the shotgun and a pair of shells from the floor. He saw his father's hat and moved to pick it up. But he stopped, stared at it a moment, and left it. He unhitched his horse from their wagon and rode west toward Barren Flats.

Chapter 9

Just before dawn, Tezcat sat at a table in a small hovel, staring at the witch. The sheriff's shotgun lay across his lap.

A fire smoldered in a pit carved into the one adobe wall of her single-room dwelling. Sand hissed through the gaps between the poorly spaced boards making up the other three walls, and weak rays of silver moonlight formed milky pools on the floor.

The bodies of Tezcat's wife and daughter lay on a pile of rotten blankets before the fire. They had begun to spoil.

The witch, Emygdia, sat across the table in a pocket of darkness, still as a corpse. Long gray hair pulled back loosely into a silver ring. Large, brown eyes. Her hands lay palms down on the table, a series of gaudy silver rings on her fingers, each emblazoned with bright jewels.

"Did you bring me what I asked?" she said.

"I have the gun, and the souls of the six men who killed my wife and daughter," Tezcat said.

The witch laughed hoarsely, and a gray, wrinkled hand unfolded from the darkness. "Give it to me," she said.

"Andréa was killed," he said.

The witch's face was stone.

"Is it true you made them beasts?"

She watched him with that stony expression.

"You could have warned us," he said.

She grinned and raised a hand toward Juana and Maria. "Shall we move on?"

"Why should I not let them rest in peace with God?" Tezcat said.

"God?" the witch said. Her dry laughter sounded from the shadows. "There is no God."

Tezcat was not sure of that. But he hoped his family was at peace. He stood, and the witch looked up at him. Her hollow eyes narrowed with dawning realization.

"Wherever they are, they are better off," he said.

Tezcat raised the shotgun to the witch's head, and as the shot sounded, sending a knot of sparrows fleeing from the barren trees outside the witch's hovel, the first orange light of dawn crept up over the horizon.

GRAVE MARKER

ADRIAN LUDENS

BOTTLED
SPIRITS

Chapter 1
A Prison of Purity

"Damn it!" Sheriff Seth Bullock pounded one palm with his fist. "Where the hell is that Indian?"

Truman Bonner gazed down the darkened passage. The two men stood waiting in the earthen tunnel. "He'll be here."

"He damn well better be," Bullock growled. "Sister Mary isn't going to last much longer. If anything, the damp atmosphere down here has sped up the process."

Truman squinted into the darkness.

"If this doesn't work, then God have mercy on us all," Bullock said.

"And if it does work?"

The sheriff seemed to consider, then looked Truman square in the eye. "Let God have mercy on us either way."

"What happened to the miner who found this?"

Bullock gave Truman a long look before answering. "He went after a fellow prospector with a pick axe. I had to shoot him. Found that blob dripping from the dead feller's mouth. Thought it might be a slug. Not a bullet, you know, but a slug like you find under a rock. I heard rumors that some fellers will lick toads and go plum crazy. Thought it might be like that, but —"

"But this was something different." Truman finished.

"That's the understatement of the century," Bullock said.

A figure separated itself from the shadows of the tunnel.

"Finally!" Bullock glared at the approaching Lakota medicine man. "She's fading fast."

"One of your deputies delayed me," Makohloka said. "I think he stopped my horse just because he saw my eagle feather headdress."

"We'll discuss that later. Do you have that accursed thing?"

Makohloka pursed his lips and raised the object. Truman, standing between the men, shuddered. "We'd better get moving before it's too late."

Truman, Sheriff Bullock, and Makohloka entered the nun's freshly built cell. Lantern light barely pushed back the darkness.

"Sister?" Bullock said. "We're here like you asked."

Sister Mary Agnes Gwyn opened her eyes and struggled into a sitting position. Her breaths came in short, phlegm-rattling gasps. "Makohloka, do you have the talisman?"

The dark-skinned man nodded. Sister Mary coughed, and dark, wet flecks sprayed from her mouth.

Truman couldn't hold his tongue any longer. "Sister, you don't have to do this."

The nun raised one hand in a feeble gesture that indicated she would brook no further argument. Truman closed his mouth.

"Have you made your peace with your Savior, Sister?" Bullock asked. Truman thought he sounded embarrassed.

The nun nodded. "What happens next must be done. It is my choice. I ask only that you do it quick and follow the steps as we discussed."

The medicine man raised the arrow. The arrowhead resembled obsidian, but Truman knew the truth. It moved sluggishly, like a slug found under a large rock. This creature had quite possibly climbed from the depths of hell. Truman wished he had a Bible, though what good it would do he couldn't say.

Sister Mary eased back onto the blanket spread on the hard floor. Bullock stepped back and placed his hand on the heavy cell door. Truman knew the plan. If this went wrong and the creature got loose, they would sacrifice themselves to protect others. Bullock would slam the door and lock the rest of them in.

Truman glanced once more at the arrowhead. He'd stood by when the old Chinaman, Shen Liu, the tall, bearded Preacher Smith, and Makohloka had clasped hands and each earnestly prayed in their native tongue. They'd cast a powerful spell, yet the arrowhead was already losing its shape as the defensive shield they'd created weakened. The plan was to place the imp in a second, stronger prison before it escaped from the first.

Makohloka knelt and raised the arrow over his head with both hands. Sister Mary nodded and closed her eyes, arms at her sides. He thrust the arrow down and slammed the tip through her ribs right above her heart. Her eyes flew open and blood spurted from her mouth. Makohloka bent and snapped the arrow's shaft, leaving the obsidian-like tip of corruption inside the nun's convulsing body.

"Time to go," Truman urged the Lakota holy man. The pair hurried out of the cell and Bullock followed, slamming the door behind them. He turned the key in the lock just as Sister Mary unleashed a scream so loud that it overwhelmed Truman's eardrums. Tears spilled from his eyes. Bullock staggered and covered his ears with his hands. Makohloka, the color drained from his cheeks, mouthed an incantation Truman couldn't hear. Bullock pinched his bandanna to his nose, which had begun to trickle droplets of blood.

Truman slid the eyehole open for one last look. Sister Mary flew against the bars with brute force that shook dirt from the ceiling of her improvised cell. Blood and spittle sprayed from her mouth and her fingernails raked at her chest.

"You sheep-molesting bastards," a voice croaked. "Let me out! It burns inside this innocent bitch!"

Chapter 2
Possessed by Spirits

Truman left one possessed woman for another.

He rode his buckskin, Prior, from Deadwood to his home in Sturgis after the caging of the perverse imp. He gazed through the spruce at the stars above and let his pony follow the trail. The night sky above put Truman in a mood both inquisitive and introspective. Had the imp come from one of the stars twinkling innocently in the night sky, or from somewhere deep in the bowels of the earth? Perhaps it had come from within, he mused. What if the imp was a physical manifestation of the dark potential within each member of the human race? He hoped their solution would prove to be a permanent one.

Prior chewed up the miles with long strides of his dark brown legs. Truman had left Deadwood just after midnight. He and Prior approached the Bonner homestead nestled on the western edge of Sturgis just before dawn.

A ghostly white face rose out of the darkness and Truman drew his Colt .45. Prior did not shy away from the sudden apparition, and after a moment, Truman saw why.

"Isaac!" he addressed his son. "What are you doing up at this hour? And why are you out here instead of inside, asleep?"

"Ma's been drinkin' again," the boy said. His brown hair stood up in a cowlick, and purple crescents hung under eyes. "She got herself some sour mash from one of the neighbors, I think."

Truman felt something twist in his heart. A boy Isaac's age should only have the vaguest idea of liquor. The situation set Truman's teeth on edge. He dismounted and handed the reins to his son.

"Get Prior unsaddled and stalled with plenty of fresh hay and water in his trough." He ruffled the boy's brown hair. "I'll go see about your mother."

Isaac led the horse to the barn. Truman headed toward the house, his boots crunching gravel with each purposeful stride. He pushed open the door. From inside the main room came the sound of ragged snoring. Helena Bonner — once Helena Flynn, still a feisty, opin-ionated young woman from the Emerald Isle — lay sprawled on the pine slats of the floor.

Truman knelt next to her and sighed. Helena had smarts that equaled any schoolmarm in the Dakota Territory, and impish good looks that rivaled any Deadwood dance hall girl, but when deep in drink, she transformed into something ugly and mean. An empty mason jar lay on the floor beside her auburn curls. Another sat empty upon the rough-hewn table. A tell-tale wet stain covered part of the log cabin's wall, beneath which were the shattered remnants of a third jar. Tru-man pictured Isaac narrowly avoiding the thrown jar and his thoughts darkened.

He leaned over his wife and slapped her cheek. Helena snorted and turned her face away. Truman crawled and put one knee on the folds of her gingham skirt between her legs. He didn't want her to roll away until he'd had his say. Something cold and wet soaked through the fabric of his trousers where he'd knelt. Truman gritted his teeth in self-righteous fury.

"Wake up, damn it." He shook her until her eyes fluttered open, bloodshot and watery.

Helena mumbled something that may have been "What do you want?" Her eyes drifted shut, but Truman slapped her other cheek.

"What?" Helena sounded angry, as if he was the one staggering home at the break of dawn, drunk as a skunk and mean as a snake. After the things he'd seen and been a part of, this infuriated him more than anything.

"If you're going to lie in your own filth like an animal," Truman growled, "then you can sleep in the barn like an animal, too."

Adrenaline infused his limbs with strength, and he hoisted his intoxicated spouse over his shoulder. He stomped across the floor and out into the chilly gray dawn. Hints of pink colored the clouds in the east.

"Truman, put me down." Helena slapped his back.

"You went and got liquor again, after I forbade it!" An idea occurred to him. "Do you know where Isaac was when I got here?"

"In bed?" Helena didn't sound sure.

"He fell down the well," Truman spat. "I got here just in time to save him, no thanks to you and your drunken shenanigans."

"You're a liar."

They'd entered the barn and Truman found an empty stall. "And you're pathetic." He threw Helena into the bedding of straw and turned away.

"Why are you treating me like this? I haven't done anything wrong."

"Sleep it off. Then we're going in to Sturgis to see the Reverend. Maybe he can help you see the truth, since you won't hear it from me."

He left the barn and latched the door. Isaac stood in the yard, waiting. Concern etched lines into his face. Truman squeezed his son with a one-armed hug and guided him toward the house.

"She just needs to be taught a lesson. Things will get better after this, I promise."

But six hours later, when Truman re-entered the barn to find Helena gone, he realized she'd made him a liar.

Chapter 3
Dealt a Bad Hand

Near the top of a mountain he didn't remember climbing, Truman Bonner approached an area where the spruce and pine needles and other brush had been cleared away, exposing the dark earth. A sweat lodge constructed of tree branches and tanned buffalo hides sat in the center of the cleared area. The remains of a fire smoldered a few yards away, and Truman noted a pair of stray stones still heating in the embers. A Lakota man stepped out of the sweat lodge and raised his hand in a somber greeting. "*Hau, kola*," he said as Truman approached. "Hello, friend."

Truman responded in kind. "*Hau, kola*. I am Truman Bonner."

"*Micaje Nape Sica*. My name is Bad Hand."

"Are you alone, or are there others?"

"I am *esnella* — a loner. I come to *Paha Sapa* because my heart cries for a vision."

Truman nodded, feeling an immediate kinship with the other man. Though the colors of their skin differed, Truman noted that they shared the same eye color: the rich brown of a dark bay horse. "I seek a vision as well. My wife, Helena, left our home in Sturgis. We had … words. My son and I have been following her trail, but the trail has grown cold."

He looked around and realized Isaac was nowhere in sight.

Bad Hand gestured for Truman to enter the sweat lodge. The cowboy ambled forward.

"*Iyotaka*," Bad Hand said when they were inside, motioning Truman to sit. Heated stones from the fire pit outside filled a shallow pit in the center of the enclosure. Truman stripped off his shirt and waited for his eyes to adjust to the dark interior. Bad Hand positioned himself opposite, pouring water onto the stones. Steam billowed and Truman fought the feeling of claustrophobia that welled within him. After several minutes, Bad Hand repeated the procedure with the water. He next removed a small clay pipe from a leather pouch and filled it with sacred tobacco. Bad Hand chanted a prayer and smoked. Truman waited, sweating and trying to keep his mind clear. He wiped droplets away from his brow, conscious of the deepening lines of worry taking root there. Finally, Bad Hand passed the pipe across the stones and sat back.

"We are on *ki wanagi tacaku*, the spirit path," Bad Hand announced.

Truman frowned. He raised the pipe to his lips with tremulous hands. He inhaled and his lungs felt scorched. Another inhalation and his lungs cooled. A sense of peace washed over him. He handed the pipe back. Bad Hand closed his eyes and began a chant.

Truman's ears hummed. He remained still and tried to relax, but

GRAVE MARKERS, VOLUME 3

felt as if he might melt in the heat. Even in darkness, shadows seemed to flit around the sweat lodge. The humming sound grew to an unbearable roar.

"PAAAAA!"

Then silence.

Truman looked not at a vision of his wife as he had hoped, but at his lanky son. Isaac hung from a tree, his hands lashed to a sturdy branch by unseen bonds. He realized his son had been shouting for him. "Find me, Pa, before it's too late!"

The cowboy blinked and found himself back in the sweat lodge. Bad Hand still chanted across from him. As Truman watched, the other man's eyelids fluttered and opened.

"I have seen both of our futures; one grim, the other grimmer still. A holy man will die tomorrow. I will pay the ultimate price. Soon my spirit will go to *Mahpiya*, to Paradise, but not to stay. It is good that we met here in the Spirit World."

Truman didn't know what to say, so he kept silent.

"I have done no wrong," Bad Hand said. "My heart is good, though I could have lived a better life. *Wakan Tanka*, the Great Spirit, has chosen for me a new quest. Go, Truman Bonner. First, you must find your son. Then I will join you on your greater journey. Find me again in Deadwood, at the Gem Saloon."

Bad Hand raised both arms, elbows out, thumbs under his chin. He lifted his head off of his neck, hefted it like a small boulder, and tossed it into Truman's lap.

Chapter 4
Long in the Tooth

Truman awoke with a strangled cry. He sat up and rubbed his eyes. His muscles protested and his joints felt stiff from sleeping rough. Bad Hand and the sweat lodge were gone. The entire landscape had changed.

"I just had the strangest dream ..." Truman broke off and looked around. They'd made camp on the edge of a small meadow bordering on a thick stand of trees. Prior and Addie, Isaac's golden Palomino, had been hobbled and munched grass contentedly. The sun had changed position. It had warmed his shoulders as they had eaten, but now it had begun to sink beneath the horizon. Glowing embers showed the remains of their campfire. Truman saw no sign of his son.

"Isaac!" Truman called. "If you can hear me, let me know!"

No response came. Had his dream contained a prophecy? Though he'd given his son a Bowie knife on his last birthday and had taught him how to use it, those skills wouldn't protect Isaac from an angry timber rattler or a fall amongst the granite outcroppings. Truman scrambled to his feet.

Truman chastised himself for dozing off; the boy had apparently given in to the temptation to explore. Long shadows tied the trees together in a web of growing darkness as Truman followed his son's footprints through the forest. The narrow path snaked between tree trunks and disappeared in the distance.

Fighting to remain calm, Truman advanced and examined the underbrush for broken twigs, bent leaves, and other signs of recent passage. He saw prints and recognized the repairs he had done on Isaac's left boot heel. The rapid approach of a moonless night did not work in his favor; though Truman considered himself a fair tracker, he could not see in the dark.

Truman soldiered on, calling his son's name. Dusk became night, and Truman's nerves wound ever tighter. The trees seemed to part before him and close in behind him as he passed. High above, Truman made out a few stars that had taken their places in the night sky.

He looked back down and saw a figure materialize in the darkness ahead. Truman drew his Colt .45 Peacemaker.

"Ye need not fear me." The voice was that of an old woman.

Truman holstered his weapon and stepped forward, staying loose and wary.

The woman, tall and willowy of frame, appeared to be alone. She wore a long, dark cloak of rough-hewn fabric, and her features hid in the shadows of a hood. She curtsied and asked, "Whither thou goest?"

The newcomer's antiquated choice of words slowed his understanding, but after a moment Truman replied. "I am searching for my son. He wandered from our campsite. Have you seen a boy on the path? He just turned twelve, but already stands up to my chest. Curly brown hair, brown eyes, slender, talkative."

The woman appeared to shrug. "I saw a boy not long ago. Brown hair and eyes? Aye. Talkative? Nay."

Her words chilled Truman. "Where did you see him? Was he hurt?"

"Turn right at the fork in the path just ahead." She stretched out an arm and pointed. The sleeve of her cloak was so long that her hand never came into view.

Truman looked but could not discern any divergence in the path. After a moment's hesitation, he said, "Could you guide me? I need to find him soon."

He thought of his fiery Irish wife. The woman he loved, whose demons he so hated, now two weeks gone. Helena had run off, or — if Truman were to be truthful with himself — he'd run her off. Her drinking and his self-righteous anger had proven a disastrous mixture. Now his son had gone missing, too. Truman struggled against the rising panic that threatened to bust loose like a wild mustang escaping the confines of a corral.

The woman stepped nearer. "Some call me The Old Maid." Truman could not disagree. Based on her reedy voice and the webbing of deep wrinkles he could see around her eyes, she seemed to have reached an advanced age. 'Long in the tooth' was the phrase Truman's long-dead father would have used. He also realized what accounted for at least part of his trouble understanding her. Green cloth wrapped the lower portion of her face.

Seeing him looking, the Old Maid tittered. It sounded like someone shaking a leather pouch filled with shards of broken glass. "It keeps away the chill. Now, come, let us commence our brief excursion."

She turned and led the way into the smokestack blackness. The path, such as it was, narrowed even further. Branches clutched and grabbed at Truman as he passed. He kept one hand on his hat brim so he wouldn't lose it.

Truman's mind turned to Isaac and how his eyes never seemed to lose their hopeful gleam. Where feelings of guilt and loss drove Truman, Isaac simply looked forward to seeing his mother again.

"What will you say to her when we find her?" his son had asked as they'd gathered dry wood for the campfire.

The question had taken Truman off guard. He'd gazed at the trees surrounding them as if they might offer suggestions. "I'd ask her why she ran away." His own words had given him pause. Was he trying to fool his son or himself? Truman set his shoulders and plunged ahead on a course closer to the truth. "Then I'd ask her forgiveness for what I done. Tell her I was a damned fool. I'd ask her to come back."

"I'm going to tell Ma I love her," Isaac had said.

His son's words had touched Truman's heart. The boy's personality — a potent mix of innocence and wisdom — always surprised him and made him proud.

The gunshot crack of a dead branch startled Truman back to the present. The Old Maid had whirled and clawed at his face with the ferocity of a cornered mountain lion. Truman lurched and toppled over a fallen log. He spat dry, bitter pine needles from his mouth and rolled into a crouch.

His attacker threw the hood back and cast aside the cloak. What the starlight revealed appalled the cowboy. The woman's left arm was sinewy and muscular. Long nails grew like talons from that hand. Her other arm looked as if the flesh had been stripped from it, leaving only skin to mend itself around the bone. She had no right hand.

Her muscular legs, clad in deerskin leggings, looked as if they could carry her a hundred miles or more before tiring. As she came toward him, she tore the green cloth from her face. Truman stifled a scream.

The removal of the wrappings revealed a sagging jaw that hung like a broken stirrup from her face. Truman felt revolted at the sight of the sharp, wicked-looking teeth protruding from her mouth. He was sure his father had never met anyone quite so 'long in the tooth' as this hag.

Knowing he faced immediate danger, Truman reached for his .45, only to find his holster empty. She leaped upon him, used her stub to pin him to the ground, and raked at his face with her nails. This time the Old Maid's attack drew blood. Hot trickles blazed trails across his skin. Sweat immediately stung the wounds. He grunted in pain and felt the ground for his missing weapon.

The Old Maid unfurled a hideous length of tongue and lapped the rivulets of blood from his wounds. A carrion reek emanated from her maw as her tongue probed into the deepest of his facial lacerations.

The pain made the treetops above him spin like the skirts of dancehall girls.

Truman's eyes found and fixed upon a silhouetted figure dangling from a tree branch about ten yards away. He knew at a glance that it was his son. Isaac's hands were tied together and fastened to a sturdy branch. But why hadn't he called out for help?

Dread filled him, and he raked the earth with his hands, desperate to find his six-shooter. What his fingers found instead was a jagged rock. Truman seized the makeshift weapon and dashed it against the side of his attacker's skull.

Her pain-induced screech made Truman's ears ring, but he seized the opportunity to push her away. He half crawled, half scrambled along the forest floor. He heard the Old Maid skitter through the vegetation close at his heels. Truman spun around a tree trunk back toward the hag. He twisted to let her talons slash past his face, and then sent two hard punches to her midsection.

The Old Maid only laughed.

Truman clasped his hands over his head and sent a crashing blow into her leering face. She staggered and sank to the ground. Truman pressed his advantage and drove a knee into his adversary's nose. It collapsed with an audible crunch and her head jolted back. He cocked his leg for a kick, but faltered when she opened her jaws wide as if inviting this move. Teeth lined her gums like ivory knitting needles. The Old Maid whipped a leg out and took his knees out from under him. He tumbled to the ground and felt the air driven from his lungs. He also felt a solid object beneath his left forearm.

Truman fought to draw air into his deflated lungs as the Old Maid rose up with an outraged cry. Truman blindly grabbed the object and felt the bite of a blade deep in the flesh between his thumb and trigger finger. It wasn't his weapon after all. It was Isaac's — the Bowie knife.

Cool air seemed to drip into his lungs, like a slow trickle from a natural spring. The Old Maid had paused, as if cherishing the moment before plunging in for the kill. Feeling lightheaded, Truman transferred the knife to his uninjured right hand and slid so his back braced against the trunk of an aspen. The Old Maid lurched toward him. Blood trickling from the wound on her temple and her flattened nostrils added dark rivers to the already detailed parchment map of her weathered face. Her black eyes glittered atop a leering mouth that remained at the forefront of Truman's worries.

The attacker lunged through the air from six feet away and came down on him with a screech. He barely got the knife up in time, but her momentum assisted his cause, and the blade pierced her chest cleanly. He heard the wet crunch of her ribs snapping and realized that the entire left side of her chest had imploded from the force of the blade. His fist — still gripping the handle of the knife — disappeared completely, swallowed into the wound. Over her shoulder, Truman saw several inches of protruding knife blade. The blood on the steel looked black in the starlight.

The Old Maid mewled and hacked up blood. It spattered onto his face as she convulsed atop him. Her eyes rolled back in their sockets, and at last she grew still. Concern for his son now returned to the forefront of his mind. He shoved his attacker away. Truman's fist made a wet, squelching sound as he pulled it from her chest; it reminded him of the first birth of a calf he had witnessed as a boy. Using an aspen trunk for support, he stood on shaky knees. He wiped his face with his dry sleeve. It came away sticky.

Truman staggered to his son. Isaac hung by his wrists from a low-hanging pine branch. The boy's unruly curls had changed from brown to mountain goat white. Arrows of guilt riddled Truman's heart. Father stood next to son in a sideways embrace. By stretching, Truman was able to use the bent and bloody knife blade to saw through the strands the hag had used to keep Isaac captive. His son slipped from his grasp and dropped from the branch like a piece of overripe fruit.

Truman held out his good hand, and Isaac wordlessly took hold of it. Truman pulled the boy to his feet thinking it would only be a matter of time before the boy unleashed a torrent of babbled words about the incident, but he realized he'd have to be patient. Isaac had obviously received quite a shock.

"Just rest easy, Son. You're safe now, and you don't have to talk about what happened until you're good and ready."

Isaac opened his mouth, but no words came. Instead trickles of black liquid seeped from between his lips and down his chin. Isaac mimed taking a bite, chewing, and then swallowing. Truman gaped as Isaac pointed to where the hag lay and then back at his mouth.

Truman finally understood Isaac's silence, and an anguished groan escaped his lips. Isaac had looked death in the face and had lost a part of his physical self in the process. Despite the ordeal, a newfound strength seemed to be present in his son's eyes. Something familiar lingered there as well. Truman still saw a hopeful gleam in Isaac's gaze. The antici-pation of reuniting with his mother still fueled the boy's love of life.

Awestruck and heartbroken in equal measure, Truman embraced his son and wept.

Chapter 5
Miner Encounter, Major Problem

It was afternoon the next day by the time Truman and Isaac forded the stream in Spruce Gulch. They began the slow ascent of another wooded hill. The wind and trees conspired to play auditory tricks, and when they crested the hill, a startling cacophony of sounds greeted the pair. Prior tossed his head with apparent disapproval. "I know. We're back here far too soon," Truman muttered. Isaac gaped at the scene in the valley below them. The bustling cavalcade of activity at the bottom of the hill seemed to entrance him.

"Deadwood," Truman said, as if the name alone explained everything there was to explain. Isaac only nodded. They rode into town.

After the Old Maid's brutal attack, Truman had cast about in the brush until he located the cloth she had worn around her face. He had used it to bind his wounded hand, relishing the irony of his attacker's disguise becoming his tourniquet. Isaac had recovered the Colt .45 from the underbrush, and the pair had hobbled arm-in-arm back to their campsite and their horses. Truman thought it prudent to seek the services of the nearest doctor for Isaac's injury.

Men shouted, laughed, and called to one another. Grubby miners, cursing and spitting, led pack mules through the streets. Dusty cowhands tilted their heads to look up at the kept women who flirted from the windows of their rooms. Some of the men turned away while others shuffled toward the brothel doors, looking both excited and foolish. Chinese men showed obsequious smiles as they pulled their carts, disappearing like ants into dark passageways. The tinkle of a piano came from one saloon. The batwing doors of another burst open and a barkeep tossed into the dust a dapper-looking gambler who'd been caught cheating. One or two respectable women of society ventured along the streets, while legitimate businessmen and shadier characters smoked cigars and gave each other shrewd looks. A group of Lakota Sioux Indians, in town for the day to trade, made an eye-catching spectacle of buckskin and feathers.

Truman and Isaac found a painted sign indicating the office of someone named Dr. Twiley. They hitched their horses to a nearby rail and ascended the stairs. The man in question turned out to be a dentist, but he said he'd been a surgeon serving the Union during the Civil War. Truman decided to trust the man's judgment.

"The tongue heals itself," Twiley said after inspecting Isaac's mouth. "Give it a week or two. In the meantime, a nip of rye now and then will help ease his pain."

Truman thought about telling the dentist he didn't approve of spirits, but he kept silent. Twiley gave Isaac's shoulder a squeeze. "And son, like as not, you'll have to relearn eating. Take it slow, so you don't choke."

After thanking the man — the dentist refused any payment — Truman and Isaac descended the stairs and returned to the bustling street of the booming mining town.

"Excuse me," Truman said. "I'm looking for my wife." No one paid any heed. Truman raised his voice and repeated his plea. A few heads turned, but those folks lost interest after a moment and moved past. Truman walked to the center of the street and removed his .45 from his holster. He fired it in the air. Heads turned. Some people froze while others scampered away. Truman looked around, dismayed to see at least half a dozen revolvers and shotguns drawn and aimed at him and his son.

"My wife is missing, maybe in grave danger!" he shouted. "This is our son. We're asking for help finding her."

Isaac gazed steadily at his father. Truman drew strength from the boy's calm presence. No time to back down now.

"Her name is Helena," he called. "Curly red hair, freckles across her nose. Pale skin — like milk. Green eyes — like duckweed."

"How'd a beauty like that end up stuck with a skinny sodbuster like you?" someone called. Several men laughed.

"If I *did* find her, I wouldn't give her back!" This time Truman saw the speaker, a sunburned cowboy wearing wooly chaps despite the heat. He felt his lips tighten. Anger rose up within him.

Truman felt someone touch his arm and started. He looked down to find a wizened old Chinese man standing beside him where no one had been a moment earlier. Truman regarded the man. He wore a black silk jacket embroidered with white thread. His dark eyes seemed to flicker in the sunlight, and a long white mustache hung like cobwebs from both sides of his thin mouth. "I am Shen Liu. I helped you."

Truman finally recognized him. "Yes, of course! You helped with the ... special arrowhead."

The old man bowed.

"You've seen my wife?"

The old man shook his head. "No, but follow me, please."

Truman and Isaac exchanged a glance. "What about my son?"

"He comes, too."

The pair followed Shen Liu's diminutive frame until Truman saw wooden steps descending along the side of a building. Looking down, he had a momentary flashback to the events involving Sister Mary Agnes Gwyn. He thought he saw her ghostly white face floating in the darkness below, but he blinked and the apparition disappeared.

They descended the steps, and Shen Liu pushed open a red-painted wooden door. The trio stepped into a dark stone passageway lit by lanterns that hung from nails in the walls and were positioned every twenty yards or so. Truman moved cautiously along the chilly passage, keeping Isaac close. Ahead of them, the rumble of a wooden laundry cart grew and then faded away until Truman heard only their footsteps on the packed earth and the gentle hiss of the oil lamps.

Shen Liu led them down a different passage, one so small that Truman had to stoop to enter, though Isaac followed with ease. They trailed the old man down the pitch black tunnel. Their guide told them when to turn left or right or when there was a step up or down. After a period of prolonged travel, Truman began to feel claustrophobic.

"Where are you taking us?" he muttered. "I'm a cowpuncher searching for my wife, not a miner searching for the mother lode."

A hand grabbed the back of Truman's collar and hauled him backward into a dimly lit den. He spun around and reached for his .45, but he was shocked to find his holster empty. On the verge of panic, Truman realized Shen Liu stood in front of him brandishing his gun.

"You are slow," the Chinese man said. He handed back the gun. Truman took it, stupefied. Behind him, Isaac peered into the room. The old man gestured toward a luxuriant rug. "You lose your wife, but are not a miner. A miner knows about your wife, but he is lost himself. Very strange. You help each other, yes? Sit please."

Isaac eased himself to the floor and sat cross-legged before a wooden tray. Ivory inlays and opalescent seashells decorated the tray. Atop the wooden tray were a variety of items: two smaller metal trays, a tiny oil lamp, and a pipe with a bamboo stem and a blue and white porcelain bowl. The old man sat down across from Isaac.

Alarmed, Truman stooped and pulled Isaac back to his feet. "An opium den is no place for a boy."

Shen Liu said nothing. He trimmed the wick on the little oil lamp. The old man filled a pipe using something that looked to Truman like a skeleton key with a tiny spoon at one end. Shen Liu raised his pipe to his lips and inhaled deeply. He closed his eyes and his shoulders sank as he relaxed.

"We build tunnels for laundry business, but have many secret places." The old man arched an eyebrow at Truman as smoke swirled within the dim alcove.

Truman thought again of Sister Mary's cell, but said nothing.

"A terrible crime happened in Deadwood, then another. Evil men flee. Where they go, I do not know. Only luck that I hear you in the street, asking."

Truman shifted his weight from one foot to the other. "How does the miner figure in?"

"This miner, Clarence Conroy, found a letter as he reached the Black Hills. Someone put pages under a rock. The fool thought he found a map to hidden gold. He came into my emporium. I heard him complaining about his bad luck."

Shen Liu had closed his eyes, lost in reverie.

"I own the Dragon Emporium. My wife and I sell food, spices, and medicines imported from China. They are true luxuries. The miner read the pages out loud. The writer reveals the outlaws' names. This Conroy decided he wanted reward for the pages. We send for Sheriff, but he did not come right away. My wife prepared delicious soup for miner. He eats, loses himself. You help him, and then he helps you."

Truman frowned. "I don't follow."

Shen Liu held the pipe over the flame, then returned it to his lips. "The first terrible crime happened here in Chinatown. My wife tried to help. Miner got the wrong soup."

Father and son exchanged glances. Isaac shrugged. Truman felt like shrugging in response. Instead, he asked, "How is my wife involved?"

Shen Liu retired to a corner of the little room. He twirled one end of his wispy mustache with a long-nailed finger.

"At the bottom of the pages is name: Helena Flynn Bonner."

Truman's pulse raced. Had Helena fallen in with a band of out-laws? Or had she been taken by force? His guts rolled like a snake uncoiling from its den. He swallowed hard, the dry click sounding in the crypt-like silence of the room.

"How can I help?"

"The cell," Shen Liu said. "You must take the miner to the cell in-habited by the *yāomó*, the demon."

Truman shuddered at the prospect. Cold sweat broke out across his forehead. He wiped his face with a bandanna. "Why don't you do it?"

"I have much to lose; you have much to gain."

Truman felt the blood drain from his face. He leveled his gaze at the old man for nearly a minute.

"Where is the miner now?" Truman said at last.

Chapter 6
Ghost Soup

Truman Bonner grunted from the effort as he backed down one of the Chinese laundry tunnels beneath Deadwood. His son, Isaac, followed. Between them, hogtied and drenched in sour sweat, writhed the lunatic prospector, Clarence Conroy. Their captive would have been howling in protest if not for Truman's dirty bandanna wadded up in his mouth. The flickering oil lanterns nailed to support beams cast just enough light to assure them that they hadn't gone blind.

As they moved along, Truman wrestled with guilt over involving his son in such a ghastly endeavor. He had to admit that Isaac had been through worse and showed more bravery and presence of mind than most men three times his age. In truth, there was no one Truman trusted more in a situation like this.

"So nice of Shen Liu to let us use a laundry cart," Truman remarked. Isaac grinned.

Truman began to recognize cryptic sigils that he and his compatriots had inscribed on the walls. They were nearing the spot where

Sister Mary Agnes Gwyn remained covertly cloistered. Her papal enclosure was only a crude cell, its grillwork made of heavy iron bars, all of it shrouded in perpetual darkness.

Truman and Sheriff Bullock had arranged with certain members of the Chinese-immigrant community to facilitate the building of this secret prison. And all because of a perverse imp that someone, in their quest for gold, had discovered deep in a cavern.

Still carrying Clarence, Truman and Isaac shambled along until they finally reached a dead end. Truman pressed one of the stones and part of the wall receded. The cowboy lit an oil lantern he found hanging from a spike just inside the revealed entrance, then held it aloft. He looped the fingers of his free hand under the length of rope binding the prospector's wrists and lifted. The rope bit at Truman's palm. They made their way through the passage until they reached the heavy, locked door that led to the antechamber of the nun's cell. Panting, they dropped Clarence onto the dank stone floor, then Truman fed the key Shen Liu had given him into the lock. The door creaked open, and Truman approached the iron bars, lantern in hand. Behind him, he heard the sounds of shuffling boots as Isaac dragged the prospector into the chamber.

"What have we here?" The voice that came from behind the bars sent a bitter chill racing down Truman's spine, like a January wind howling across the Dakota prairie.

"This is Clarence Conroy."

"Bring him to me."

Truman hesitated. "Not yet. Someone believes you may possess the power to heal this man. He's having violent tantrums. He chased after townsfolk with a pick axe."

The figure, shrouded in a long black tunic, stood statue-like behind the bars. A black veil covered not only the nun's hair, but hid her face as well. "Your mouth is filled with lies born out of selfish concerns. I will not be lied to."

The nun turned away and made as if the lie back down in the corner of the cell.

Truman relented. "He's secreted away a journal belonging to my wife. She's missing. The journal could help us locate her, but in his current state, he's unable to help us."

"Remove the cloth from his mouth and bring him to me," the voice repeated.

Truman made brief eye contact with Isaac, and then the pair lifted the crazed man to his feet. Truman removed the makeshift gag and the skinny prospector immediately unleashed a torrent of angry sentences. Truman thought he recognized at least a couple of the words as Chinese. Clarence fixed a wide-eyed gaze on Sister Mary and fell silent.

"Ask me what ails him," directed the voice from the cell.

"What ails —?"

"I'm talking to the boy."

Truman felt his face flush. "He can't speak. No tongue."

"Sorry to hear that. Truly, I am." The nun leaned toward Isaac as if waiting for a response. When he didn't react, the nun's head swiveled back to Truman. "Is he deaf as well?"

"No. He just has a low tolerance for bullshit."

The figure behind the bars surged forward. "Tell me how it happened! I love a good story!"

"Stop wasting time!" Truman said. "We're here to help Clarence. Do you know what ails him or not?"

"Of course. This fool has ingested a bowl of ghost soup."

"Ghost soup?"

"Chinese folklore contends that digging up and boiling the bones of the dead will yield a soup of highly medicinal properties. It doesn't."

"What *does* it do?" Truman asked.

"Opens a portal for angry spirits to return to this realm. Hui ta Wong is here with us. He's wearing the body of Clarence like a shabby old suit. His confusion is strong, but his anger and hatred are stronger. He tells me outlaws — *white* outlaws — raped his wife while he watched, then murdered them both for sport."

Truman glanced at the grizzled prospector as the voice continued.

"He'd like nothing more than to kill every white man he sees if given the chance. Shen Liu's wife made the soup. He served it to Clarence here by mistake. And he duped you into serving as his errand boy."

Truman ignored the jibe. "Can you remove the spirit? Take Mister Wong out of Clarence and send his soul back where it belongs?"

"I can and I will. Bring him to me."

Truman didn't move. "Tell me what you intend to do first."

"There will be a kiss."

Truman felt his mouth fall open. "A kiss? Why?"

"I will pull the unwelcome spirit from him and save his life. The errant soul will have no choice but to return to where it came from. Then all will be as it should."

Truman looked at Clarence. "Does the dead Chinaman inside Clarence know we're talking about sending him back?"

"Would he be standing here like a docile lamb if he knew?" The figure in the cell uttered a few Chinese words, and the grubby little miner grinned.

"What did you say to him?" Truman asked.

"I offered to help him turn you inside-out and dance on your steaming entrails if he kissed me through the bars."

Truman instinctively reached for his Colt .45.

"Oh, unclench," the voice behind the bars chided. "Would you rather fight him every inch of the way?"

Truman caught Isaac's eye and they each took one of Clarence's arms and guided him to the bars.

The nun lifted her veil, revealing papery, mummified skin. It reminded Truman of the dried outer layer of a yellow onion, and his stomach clenched as the odor of dead, dried flesh reached his nostrils. Truman found himself lamenting how death and the presence of the imp had corrupted Sister Mary's visage. Hui ta Wong must have sensed the trap because he howled with terror and began writhing in an attempt to get away. Truman and Isaac braced themselves and held the smaller man against the iron.

Mary Agnes's skeletal face thrust between the bars and pressed against the raving man's lips. What looked to Truman like smoky gray syrup passed from the prospector's mouth and into the nun's. Truman felt the hair on the nape of his neck stand on end, as if it were trying to uproot and relocate to calmer climes. The miner convulsed. His eyes rolled up in their sockets. The bulging whites contrasted with the hollow pockets of darkness in the skull of the nun.

Then Sister Mary fell to her knees and reached through the bars. It took a moment for Truman to realize the emaciated fingers had torn the front of the prospector's wool trousers. Before any of the men could react, the nun had taken Clarence's member in her mouth. Truman realized Isaac had loosened his hold on the old prospector's arm. He watched the proceedings with what looked like a mixture of curiosity and dismay.

Truman, feeling both amused and revolted himself, turned his gaze to Clarence. The grizzled prospector had stopped struggling. If anything, it looked as if he'd pressed himself harder against the bars. The skeletal head bobbed, the nun's habit obscuring most of the action. Truman felt his tenuous grasp of the situation rapidly dwindling. "That's enough!"

The nun paused and pulled away just enough to favor Truman with a yellow-toothed leer. "Hui ta Wong's soul proves to be rather stubborn. It doesn't want to leave. Do you want me to coax it out or don't you?"

Truman looked away. The nun resumed her ministrations. Truman moved to Isaac and led him to the corner of the antechamber. "I don't know how this is going to play out, but I apologize that you had to see this."

Behind them, Clarence emitted a squeal of pain. Truman spun around.

"*Teeeef!*" Clarence cried. "She's scrapin' me wif her teef!" Truman realized he could understand the old man again. That meant the Chinaman's soul had left. He took a quick step forward and drew his sidearm.

Clarence had braced his grubby palms against the bars in an effort to pull away. Dark ruby rivulets of the prospector's blood dribbled down Sister Mary's bony chin. Truman realized that she did not intend to release her captive unless he intervened.

"Let him go!" Truman thrust the barrel of the .45 through the bars and against the nun's skull. "Last chance!"

The nun ignored him. Truman pulled the trigger. The sound of thunder reverberated from the walls and deafened them. Dry bone fragments exploded into the air and against the cell wall.

The nun fell away, and the prospector sagged to the ground. Truman crouched and glanced at the prospector's member. There was some blood, but the wound appeared to be superficial. Truman looked up at Clarence's slack face and closed eyes. "Is he dead?"

"He's cleansed," the figure in the cell snarled. It seemed to come from far away. Truman realized his ears still rang from the gunshot.

Truman held a hand beneath the limp man's nostrils. He felt the warmth of Clarence's ragged breathing and looked at Isaac. "Drag him out into the air, quick. Take him to a horse trough and splash water on his face."

Isaac cocked one eyebrow.

"Go ahead. I'll deal with her," Truman said.

The boy dragged the unconscious man along the stone floor. After they'd disappeared around the corner, Truman turned back to the figure in the cell.

"The Chinaman's soul: were you able to retrieve it?"

"Oh my, yes. The moment I kissed him."

Truman felt his cheeks grow hot. "But you said —."

"I lied. I just wanted to have some fun."

Rage welled up in Truman like lava, but like Bear Butte, the nearby dead volcano, his fury had nowhere to go. "Put the veil back down, for God's sake," he finally muttered.

"I do nothing for God's sake."

"Cover up, I said!"

"Does her face gall you that much?"

"It's *you* who galls me."

"How hurtful you are!" The nun yanked off her veil, then wrestled the habit up over her skull. The fabric rustled as it landed in the corner of the cell.

All that remained of Mary Agnes Gwyn now lay exposed. Truman winced. It wasn't her bleached white skeleton that galled him; it was the small, sinewy figure imprisoned in the dead nun's ribcage. The unholy creature, covered in reptilian scales and black as a mineshaft at midnight, leered at him with glittering gold eyes.

"What an ugly little cuss you are," Truman said. "And you've changed."

The imp preened. "I'm stronger now."

"What are you getting at?" Truman asked. Fingertips of dread caressed his spine. "What did you do with the soul?"

"I devoured it. Another ignorant mistake on your part and I'll have enough power to break free."

"I'll never let that happen," Truman growled. Righteous assurance rose within him like a roaring prairie fire. "Despite what happened here, despite what *you* just did, Sister Mary was innocent and pure. She made the ultimate sacrifice, letting you try to possess her body as she died. But the trap was sprung. Her soul is at rest now, and her mortal coil still serves as an effective prison for you!"

The imp gave Truman a sly look. Its talons made an abrasive sound as they scraped against the inside of her rib cage. The desire to return to Isaac came over the cowboy, sudden and strong.

"Her corpse is a cage, nothing more. And soon the cage will be *empty*," the imp said. The skeletal nun began a hideous, awkward dance, like a marionette pulled by invisible strings. From his ribcage prison, the black being gave Truman a jaunty little wave. "I'll see you again soon, and it won't be here, you can bet your life on it."

Truman spun on his boot heel. He wanted to run, but forced himself to walk. He would not give the little demon the satisfaction. The imp's laughter assaulted Truman's ears as he slammed the door and turned the key in the lock, leaving the creature in absolute darkness. He hurried through the winding passages, up the steps, and out into the cool embrace of the night.

The ringing in Truman's ears went away the next day. The echoes of the imp's laughter seemed to linger much longer.

Chapter 7
Dust Devils

"I'm much obliged," Clarence Conroy said the next morning. "It was like bein' trapped in my own head. I could see everything but couldn't move, couldn't do nothin' to help myself."

Truman had paid for a room above the Saloon No. 10 for the three of them. Conroy had slept like the dead on the floor. Truman and Isaac shared the straw-filled mattress. Though Isaac slept, Truman spent most of the night chasing his own thoughts — or being chased by them.

Conroy stretched, and Truman heard the prospector's bones creak and pop. Isaac sat on the bed looking from one man to the other.

"I'm glad we could help," Truman said. "Listen, Clarence, before you fell ill …"

Conroy nodded. "The journal I found. Yes."

"Will you take us to it?"

"No."

Truman balled his hands into fists, and then winced as the palm still healing from the Old Maid's attack flared. "We helped save you!"

The old man raised both hands in a gesture of surrender. "What I mean is I don't need to take you to the journal pages. I have them right here."

Thunderstruck, Truman could only shake his head.

Conroy sat on the edge of the bed beside Isaac and pulled the left leg of his trousers up over his boot. He dipped two grimy fingers in and withdrew several curled pages.

Truman moved the water basin from the top of the dresser to the floor. Then he took the pages from Conroy's outstretched hand and flattened them out on the dresser. His eyes devoured the words on the page with growing alarm.

* * *

August 14, 1889

Dear Journal,

I make these notes in an effort to stay sane. We've been traveling north across a vast expanse of sparsely growing grassland for what feels like days. Hunger pains cramp my stomach. Worse, no one has any liquor left. Mounting fears and frustrations have tempers flaring.

Dale Hollister is the leader of our group. I met him in Deadwood after Truman's holier-than-thou tantrum. I'd ridden Spirit from the homestead and wound up at the Gem Saloon. We shared a few drinks. Then he invited me to accompany him on a "scenic ride out of the Hills."

Two other acquaintances of his, Joseph Cagle and a young man named Jamie McCrossen, have joined us. I get the impression that these three share something of a dark history. I overheard Cagle talking with Hollister. The trio felt it necessary to leave Deadwood due to an unfortunate incident with a Chinese laundryman and his wife. I heard Hollister say, "I don't think anybody who matters will give a damn, but if it will help you rest easy, we'll light a shuck north for a while." I don't know what incident they are referring to, but I fear I have fallen in with the wrong type of men. I stay close to Hollister. He had — until recently — some fine whiskey on his person, and he's kept me safe from the others, if you get my meaning.

I suppose they are outlaws. There, I said it. Might as well be honest with myself.

Why I ever left my family behind in Sturgis, I'm not sure I can say. I know I wish to return home, but circumstances have created a situation where I feel I cannot return. Truman is a good man, but life with him bores me! It's as if he's always trying to protect me. From what, I do not know. His disapproving frown follows everything I do. Isaac is a good boy, and the memory of his face pains me awfully, but I don't doubt that he can get along without me. He's close to becoming a man anyway. They are better off without me.

Hollister leads our procession. He is followed by McCrossen, and then me as I try to scratch these words, allowing Spirit to follow at his own pace. The corpulent Cagle brings up the rear, lagging behind us. I think his poor mount may have lost a shoe.

Later: As the temperature increases, the men become more quarrelsome.

I just overheard McCrossen talking to Hollister. Some awful business about a dead preacher. Hollister and McCrossen each blamed the other for the holy man's death. But then Hollister laughed and congratulated himself on running down an Indian to take the blame. I thought they'd left town because they'd robbed someone.

I should not be here. Must be vigilant and careful.

Later: I don't know how long Cagle has been gone. The sun is still high, but water is low. The horses are close to being played out. We rode with our heads down in a useless attempt at ducking the sweltering heat. I looked back to check Cagle's progress, but the large man was nowhere to be found.

I called out to the others, and we made a brief attempt at retracing our path. We found his hat but nothing else and gave up the search. This may sound heartless, but the lack of water played fearfully on our minds. According to Hollister, if we wanted any chance at finding water, we had to keep moving. So *we press on.*

The sun hangs high in the sky. Due to some trick of the light, it looks as if it hasn't moved. Hollister has assured McCrossen and me that a sinkhole must have brought about our companion's demise. Hollister rode along side me for a time, trying to raise my spirits. I found myself wishing he had spirits of another sort to offer. I find that my irritation and discomfort grows with each minute. I suffer the ill effects of prolonged exposure to the sun as well. My skin burns, my ears ring, my head aches. I no longer feel the hunger pains, but the desire for a drink is unbearable.

The mirages are the worst. The naked trunks of large, limbless trees seem to ripple and cavort in the distance in all directions. As I watch, they disappear like salmon leaping upriver to spawn.

Later: Hollister is gone. He rode away hard and fast back the way we'd come. I don't know whether to think of him as a coward or applaud his good sense.

McCrossen drew his six-shooter and shouted for Hollister to stop, but to no avail. Then he turned his weapon on me and accused me of leading them toward a sheriff's posse. I told him I'd done nothing of the sort and pointed out that Hollister had been leading us. McCrossen made me ride ahead of him, following Hollister back in the direction of Deadwood. He said if a posse waited in ambush ahead, then Hollister had the right idea by going back. I didn't know what to say to that logic. McCrossen also said if we ran into any trouble, he'd gun me down without hesitation.

Later. I write this after the fact. Here is what happened:

McCrossen still groused behind me. Then a hole in the earth opened on the path in front of me. Spirit reared back on his hind legs and threw me into the dust. Something emerged from the hole and snatched my horse away.

It looked like a mouth.

McCrossen pulled me onto his horse and urged it into a gallop in hopes of leaving this cursed stretch of land behind us, but the horse soon slowed, too played out to run any farther. It felt as if we moved at a snail's pace.

I realized then that the mirages were not mirages at all.

They look like dust devils tearing at the sand, but rather than disappearing into the sky, they sink back into the ground. Like termites overrun a dead log, something unholy infests this stretch of deserted land.

I need a drink so badly.

Water would be nice, too.

Later: McCrossen threw me off of his horse. I landed hard but managed to avoid serious injury. Perhaps I'm getting used to falling.

I know that I am in great danger. McCrossen rides ahead muttering to himself. He has revealed the awful truth about the Chinese laundry couple. All three played a part in that horror. And according to McCrossen, it was Hollister's idea to kill the preacher, too. He keeps waving his pistol around and looking back at me in a way that scares me. I think he called me the Angel of Death. He could leave me behind, yet he does not. Is he too terrified to test his own theory? Or perhaps he feels as if he deserves this hell. Perhaps we both do.

I scratch these words to pass the time and keep my mind off my own fears.

I believe one of the dust devils will come for one of us at any moment. They dive, you see. They swim through the sand, and then open up the ground beneath their prey.

McCrossen doesn't realize all this yet, but I do, and perhaps I can use this to my advantage. He rides ahead on his horse. I believe he's put himself at a deadly disadvantage.

Weight may be the key to my survival. Tread lightly, Helena.

There is some good news: I believe the temperature may have dropped a degree or two. Even better, I see in the distance a most welcome sight: the Black Hills. We're close to home!

Later: McCrossen tried to leave me behind. He sank his spurs into his horse's flanks, hoping to leave me to my fate.

Instead, the sand became a whirling vortex beneath him. McCrossen and his terrified pony were sucked down and away. I was alone.

Trembling, I sat down to inscribe this final entry. I remain as still as possible. The sun sinks low now, and this hellish day will soon come to an end. The safety of the stony foothills is close.

I am, as my overprotective Truman often commented, a 'little slip of a thing.' I believe I can make it over the last bit of desert without attracting attention from the dust devils, or whatever they truly are. Then, perhaps, I can go about finding a town, and in that town, a saloon.

I have a good feeling about my chances. It's nothing I can present facts to support, it's just a feeling. Call it a woman's intuition.

In haste, as the last of daylight dims,

Helena Flynn Bonner

Chapter 8
A Boon in a Boomtown

"That sumbitch there kilt Preacher Smith!"

The burly bartender at the Gem Saloon in Deadwood pointed with his chin toward the far end of the bar. The scent of fresh sawdust mixed with the sour tang of vomit and the cloying perfume of the soiled doves who worked in the bedrooms upstairs. Truman Bonner turned his still-healing face in the direction indicated by the speaker.

"Dirty Injun kilt the most God-fearin' man in town." The bartender scowled his disapproval. "But vengeance is mine sayeth the Lord, or at least sayeth my boss, Al Swearingen. He put a bounty on the head of Preacher Smith's murderer. A posse brought that in to prove they got him. Found him skulking around the edge of town where Preacher Smith died. Drinks were on the house for those fellers. Say what you want about Al Swearingen; the man sure knows how to get a head!" The barkeep slapped a filthy towel on the wooden bar and brayed laughter.

Truman said nothing. He paid the man for a bottle of rye for

Isaac's medicinal use and strolled to the far end of the bar for a look. The bartender had not indicated a man, but a large glass jar. It was a one-gallon size, perhaps once holding milk, pickles, or boiled eggs. Now a human head, brown and misshapen, was its only content. Coarse black hair floated like tendrils in the fluid surrounding it.

"He ought to be happy," the bartender called. "He's pickled in ninety proof!" A few grizzled miners laughed, and Truman forced a wan smile. He reached out and turned the jar with his fingertips. The decapitated head's features came into view. The eyelids popped open and Truman jolted in shock and recognition.

Truman Bonner, I'm glad you finally came. Get me away from these fools.

"Bad ..." The stunned cowboy began to speak aloud but stopped. *Bad Hand?*

Yes.

The lips did not move, but Truman felt as if he heard every word in his own native tongue. He sent a thought back. *How is this possible?*

This is your spirit path, as it is mine. Our paths have converged.

Truman glanced around the bar. The few other patrons paid no attention to him, and the barkeep had busied himself with the task of smearing his filthy towel inside each of the saloon's shot glasses. Truman found himself wondering if all of this was another dream. After all, he'd never encountered Bad Hand in real life.

As if in response, the head in the jar locked its eyes on his. *We met before in the spirit realm. You seek your beloved, Helena. She is with the men who murdered me. This much I know.*

Truman felt strange, as if his blood had become an icy slush that his heart struggled mightily to keep moving. *Where are they?*

Northwest of this place. Take me with you and we may yet help each other.

Truman closed his eyes. Was he going mad? Suffering a breakdown brought on by the stress of Helena's desertion? Perhaps. And yet, after all he'd seen and been a party to in the past few weeks, Truman wasn't inclined to dismiss anything.

Shen Liu had led him to Clarence Conroy. The miner had found Helena's journal pages. The author described unbelievable horrors, but the details about their location seemed to match what Bad Hand had just revealed.

He reopened his eyes and looked again at Bad Hand. The Lakota's eyes were now closed. Seeing the bartender engaged in garrulous conversation with a pair of just-arrived ranch hands, Truman reached out and lifted the heavy jar, stowing it in the crook of his good arm. Then he grabbed the bottle of rye with his bandaged hand. Pain lanced from the wound in his palm up to his elbow, but Truman kept his fingers curled around the bottle's neck; his son needed what the bottle contained. He turned and hurried through the saloon. To his own ears, his boots pounded the wooden slats like galloping hooves. The beckoning sky outside the batwing doors seemed to shrink to a pinpoint, too far to ever be reached. Truman mentally prayed to escape the barkeep's notice.

Better he had kept his prayers to himself. "Hey! Come back with that!" The bartender's mouth hung open in dismay.

Truman broke into a run and burst through the Gem Saloon's entrance. His eyes lit on Isaac waiting with the horses. The boy saw him and immediately unwound both sets of reins from the hitching post. As Truman ran, Isaac put a booted foot in the stirrup and swung his leg over Addie. Truman jumped from the boardwalk and held out the bottle of rye.

"Just gargle and spit," was all Truman said as Isaac took it. He vowed to caution his son about the evils of alcohol later. Right now they had to clear the street before the angry barkeeper caught up with them. Truman switched the jar containing the head to his left arm, grabbed the saddle horn with his good hand and put his foot in the stirrup. An angry shout from behind him gave Truman all the incentive he needed to leap into the saddle. He gathered Prior's reins and turned in time to see twin black holes so close to his face that they seemed to fill his entire field of vision.

"What in Sam Hell are you doin', cowboy?" the barkeep asked from the painless end of the shotgun. "That's the property of the Gem Saloon."

"Preacher Smith was a friend. And so was this man." Truman said these words not for the brawny man's benefit, but for Isaac, who had cocked an inquisitive eyebrow at the jar's contents. "I don't believe he committed any crime. He's not a mongrel or a trophy, but a good and gentle man who deserves a proper burial."

"He's a murderer, and you're a thief," the barman said. Truman thought he meant to say more, but the fellow stopped short at the metallic click of a hammer being cocked. Truman glanced at Isaac. The boy's white hair gleamed in the sunshine. His face remained emotionless. The barrel of the Colt .45 rested against the barman's temple.

Isaac had leaned over and taken it from Truman's holster while the two men spoke.

"You willing to lose your life for somethin' that you consider a novelty piece?" Truman asked. "My son and I have been through some harsh trials lately. He got his tongue bit off by a cannibal woman we encountered in the forest a few days ago. If you killed me, he wouldn't think twice about sending a bullet right through your brains. Then you 'n me could race to 'our Father who art in Heaven' and to try to explain to Him how this all happened."

The bartender's cheeks took on an ashen hue. "Mebbe we all count to three and go about our business."

"Wise choice."

The barman eased the shotgun away from Truman's face, and Isaac responded in kind. The people of Deadwood — grubby miners with their pack mules, sunburned cowhands, Chinese men pulling their laundry carts, and even a few hardy pioneer women — ventured along the streets, doing their best to ignore the gun-brandishing pair.

"I'd clear out if I were you. Al Swearingen will be awful hot when he finds out someone took his prized specimen."

Truman didn't argue with good advice. He stowed the jar in his saddle bag, then he and Isaac turned their horses and rode north out of Deadwood. After they'd left the last of the mining camp tents at the edge of town behind them, Truman removed the jar and gazed at Bad Hand. *Are they close? Is my wife hurt?*

Though he received no response, Truman hoped he'd hear from his new trail companion soon. Helena could not be far; he could not let himself believe otherwise. But who was she with and under what circumstances? These questions haunted him. He stowed the jar again and took up Prior's reins. They rode silently as the sun lengthened the shadows around them.

After an hour, Truman glanced back at his son. Isaac rode easy in the saddle, his face impossible to read. Truman was struck again by how much his son's ordeal had changed him, physically, and in the way he now carried himself.

The sun slipped behind the mountain. Soon they'd reach the place Helena had described in her writings — and what then? Truman clung to the reins, pondering. The air cooled, serving as a harbinger of the coming darkness.

Chapter 9
Betrayal Begets Betrayal

Helena languished on a bed in one of the rooms of the Franklin Hotel on the south edge of Deadwood. A potent mix of liquor and laudanum fogged her mind and weighted down her limbs. She gazed across the room at the window. Hollister had drawn the curtain not out of consideration for Helena's rest, but because he wanted to keep her away from prying eyes. She heard flies buzzing against the glass in a futile attempt at finding freedom. Helena knew they'd die there. A bottle of rye was balanced on her chest. She noticed a stray fly had found its way into the bottle. It floated in the amber liquid. Would a dead fly stop her from finishing the bottle? She doubted it.

Hollister had been waiting for her. She'd outwitted McCrossen and evaded the dust devils, only to be bushwhacked by the man who'd abandoned her.

He'd celebrated by having his way with her with sadistic brutality and then threatened her life if she tried to escape. They rode his horse back to town, where he'd taken this room and encouraged her to drown her shame with drink. Satisfied that her spirit had been broken, he'd left her, turning the key in the lock from the outside to keep her confined — a fly in a bottle.

You could run the race, fight the good fight, but what was the point when the odds were stacked against you? She took another swallow. The fly disappeared.

* * *

Dale Hollister sat alone in Saloon No. 10 drinking and listening. At an adjacent table, a miner conversed with drunken enthusiasm surrounded by compatriots.

"I saw a dungeon. A witch of enormous power is imprisoned there!"

"Shut up, Clarence, you're sloshed."

"It's true!" the first miner protested. "I seen her with my own eyes!"

Hollister tossed back the last of his drink and sidled over to the miner. "I believe you."

The older man glanced up in apparent surprise. "You do?"

Hollister leaned in and murmured. "Ten dollars in gold if you take me to her."

The miner stood up so quick he tipped his chair over with a clatter.

* * *

"We getting close, pardner?" Hollister had followed Clarence

100

around the laundry tunnels for just about as long as he cared to endure. The old man had blundered around, hitting dead ends, doubling back, making whispered assurances.

"She's hid good, but I'll find her," Clarence said. "Don't worry."

"Oh, I never worry."

The pair rounded a corner and came face to face with a little old man with a long white mustache. He wore black silk and shook a long-nailed finger in admonishment.

"You two are louder than stampeding bison."

Clarence drew back in alarm. "You! I don't want any more soup. Never again!"

Hollister took advantage of the momentary distraction and drew one of his Colt M1894s. The old Chinaman turned to flee, but Hollister darted out a hand and caught his braid.

"Hold on, little fella. I need you to be my guide." He cocked the gun and placed the barrel against the back of the old man's head. "The nun. Take us to her."

The old man led the procession through the maze of tunnels. At an apparent dead end — Hollister thought they'd been here at least once before — Liu pressed one of the stones and part of the wall receded. The Chinaman lit an oil lantern hanging from a spike and held it aloft. They made their way through the passage until they reached a heavy door. Liu slid a key into the lock and pushed the door open. He approached the iron bars, lantern in hand. Hollister followed, along with Clarence.

"Shen Liu and Clarence Conroy!" said a voice from the shadows of the cell. "Why, what a delightful surprise! And who's this tall drink of water?"

Hollister watched a figure garbed in a nun's attire rise out of the darkness.

"What are you, lady?" he asked.

"Well, I'm certainly no lady!" the figure said, somehow malicious and lascivious at the same time.

Hollister found himself becoming aroused. Dark power radiated from the prisoner. He felt it — and he craved it. He kicked the door to the antechamber closed with one booted heel and used the barrel of his gun to direct the miner and Chinaman into the far corner.

"Let's talk," Hollister said. "I assume you want out of here. I might be able to help, but the question I have is: what's it worth to you?"

From within the cell, he heard the sound of leathery wings unfurling; the nun was laughing. "You want something in return. What could that be, I wonder."

Hollister wet his lips. He was on to something big, he could feel it. "Power. A share of your power."

The nun nodded. "The bars imprison the nun. The nun imprisons me. I need strength. I need souls. I believe two will be sufficient."

Hollister eyed the pair standing in the corner. "These two?"

"Yes, bring my old friend Clarence over first."

Hollister grabbed him and dragged him to the bars. "You know this old coot?"

Again, the nun nodded. "He and I have been intimately involved."

The miner blanched and muttered protests that both outlaw and nun ignored.

"What now?" Hollister asked.

The nun drew back her veil and thrust her mummified cadaverous face through the bars. "Shoot him in the head!"

Hollister pulled the trigger. A deafening report filled the tiny room. Bits of bone, flesh, and brain sprayed against the near wall. Hollister watched the nun reach through the bars and grasp the old miner to keep him from falling. She sucked what looked like thick yellow smoke from the mouth of the dying man. Hollister ejaculated.

The nun dropped the dead miner. "Now, the second."

Hollister turned to the far corner, but the Chinaman had disappeared. He scanned the tiny room, thunderstruck. He'd stood between the old man and the door they'd entered the entire time. "How?"

"Doesn't matter," the nun said. "New plan." She reached for him through the bars and pulled him close.

"How's your gag reflex, cowboy?"

* * *

Five miles to the north, Truman and Isaac pondered the deserted expanse before them. They'd found no trace of Helena or the others she'd written about. No campfires or smoke on the horizon. The events detailed in the journal were dated several days prior. Were they too late? Dejected, Truman decided to camp for the night and return to Deadwood at dawn to inform Sheriff Bullock. Perhaps he could help them organize a posse or search party.

Chapter 10
Bottles Get Emptied

The day dragged past. Nightfall came, but Hollister never returned. Helena emptied the bottle. She dozed fitfully, her sleep interrupted by nightmares. Clouds obscured the moon. To Helena, the passage of time seemed interminable, a kind of purgatory. At last the sun began to rise. Helena did not. Pounding pain made her cover her head with the dirty sheet. Her brain felt too big for her skull. She ached, battered and raw. And something, she reflected, was missing. Something integral. Helena frowned and chewed on her lip, trying to remember what she'd lost.

She dozed. Then something happening in the street below woke her. A disturbance of some sort. She heard someone shouting. Then gunshots. A few at first, followed by a cacophony. Helena slid from the bed and tottered to the window. She moved the curtain. Looking down upon the street, she saw carnage. Bodies lay strewn. She recognized the source of the violence: Hollister, a revolver in each hand, bellowing and shooting.

Then Helena saw what she had lost. She stepped away from the window and let the curtain drop.

* * *

Truman and Isaac returned to Deadwood dispirited and exhausted. Though the horses had rested and cropped grass contentedly, neither Truman nor Isaac could sleep. After a few hours, Truman had covered their campfire with dirt and the pair had saddled the horses. They'd returned to Deadwood with the sun and rode to the Sheriff's Office to await Bullock's arrival.

One of his deputies saw them waiting and approached.

"Help you?" He spit a stream of tobacco juice into the dust.

"I'm Truman Bonner; this is my son, Isaac. I've helped Sheriff Bullock in the past. I need his help finding my wife. I believe she's been taken by force by outlaws."

The deputy nodded and spat again. "There've been terrible goings-on here lately. Not the way the sheriff wants things to be in Deadwood. Folks forgetting how to act civilized."

Truman, watch out! He's coming. The voice came to him urgent and clear. Truman excused himself from the deputy and returned to Prior. He opened his saddlebag and looked inside. Within his gallon jar, Bad Hand had reopened his eyes.

Who's coming? Truman sent the thought back as he pretended to rummage around in the saddle bag. *Bullock?*

He's coming, too; they all are. Bad Hand's features were emotionless, but his thoughts came at Truman so fast and strong that they felt like shouts. *Many spirit paths will intersect, as foretold in the vision we shared. The Great Spirit flies over us now, searching for souls.*

Isaac tugged on his father's arm. Truman looked up and saw Sheriff Bullock riding toward them from the south end of the street.

"Truman Bonner!" A cry came from the shadows across the street. Father and son turned to look. Shen Liu trotted across the road toward them. The sharp report of a gun being fired pierced the morning air. The little man threw his arms up and tumbled to the dirt.

HE'S HERE! Bad Hand warned. *My killer! But now he's —*

Anything else he wanted to convey was lost in a hailstorm of lead.

Dale Hollister walked down the center of Main Street devoid of conscience, unfettered by fear; something else had taken control. He fired matching Colt m1894s with preternatural skill and precision.

The deputy raised a Winchester rifle. Hollister pulled the trigger and took off the young lawman's hat. The top of his skull went with it.

Sheriff Bullock spurred his horse forward, drawing his gun. Hollister shot the horse out from under the approaching sheriff, sending him sprawling.

"Isaac, here!" Truman tossed his Colt .45 to the boy. Then he knelt and picked up the deputy's Winchester. He tucked the butt of the rifle against his shoulder and fired a hurried shot. Hollister didn't even flinch.

"Get behind the horses!" Truman urged. Isaac did as he was told, his features calm. Truman tried to emulate his son's demeanor, but it felt as if the world had gone insane.

Any early rising townsfolk had scattered. Bullock crawled in the dust. Truman saw that the sheriff had lost his weapon. Hollister closed in fast, still firing. Slugs kicked up geysers of dirt in the street, each one closer to the sheriff than the last.

"Shoot that man!" Truman shouted at Isaac. His son required no further urging or explanation. He began squeezing off shots at Hollister. Truman chambered another round and did the same.

The big man turned his attention from Bullock to the Bonners, grinning. A tongue of flame belched from each barrel of Hollister's guns. One slug spun Truman around and drove him to his knees. Another tore through Prior's throat.

Truman's horse toppled, its throat spurting gouts of blood. Bullock continued to crawl toward his sidearm. Addie broke free and ran. Isaac knelt to reload, and father and son realized simultaneously that Hollister had them dead to rights. Prior finished his fall and Bad Hand's jar rolled free. Truman fumbled for the Winchester but realized the ammunition he needed to reload sat inside the sheriff's office. He glanced down and saw a wet patch of crimson where the slug had grazed his shoulder. Isaac stood up. Hollister stopped and faced him not ten yards away. Truman considered hurling his hat at the man; anything to draw fire, anything to save his son.

Isaac did not appear concerned. He seemed *interested*. The boy looked at something Truman couldn't see. He felt only astonishment as his son, facing the gun-wielding outlaw alone and unarmed, broke into a grin.

* * *

Helena took a huge swig from the bottle of 90 proof and tapped Hollister's shoulder. He turned, and she spat the whiskey in his face. Then she sloshed the rest of the bottle's contents over his shoulders and across his chest in a crude parody of a baptismal cross. He allowed her ministrations for only a moment before swatting her away with a slash of one scorching hot Colt barrel, then turned to face his adversaries.

Hollister might have understood Helena's intentions, but he'd relinquished control. The imp only understood the purpose of the firearms, and the intentions of the men wielding them. He knew of only one purpose for alcohol.

Later, Helena would have time to reflect and be amazed at the strength instilled in her at seeing her husband and son in danger in the street below. For years, she would look back and marvel at how easily she'd tipped the heavy dresser sideways, destroying the brass doorknob, and escaping the room at a run. She'd reminisce about the look of shock on the bartender's face as she'd vaulted over the bar.

She'd snatched a bottle of 90-proof whiskey and a fresh-lit oil lamp from one of the tables before racing out the batwing doors.

It was this second item that she hurled at Hollister once he'd turned his back.

* * *

Truman watched as silent blue flames engulfed the outlaw's torso. The gunman bellowed and spun around like a bucking bull, trying to throw off whatever was tormenting it. His heart seemed to have stopped beating as the lumbering man changed directions and headed straight toward Isaac. The boy stumbled back, and for one heart-stopping moment, Truman felt sure that, even on fire, Hollister would gun his son down.

Then the outlaw's booted heel came down on something, and Truman saw the gunman's ankle twist like the broken neck of a soon-to-be-butchered chicken. Truman heard something pop just before Hollister collapsed.

Truman rose to his knees for a better angle. He saw three things in rapid succession: Bad Hand's jar beneath the outlaw's outstretched broken ankle; something black and viscous crawling from the burning man's mouth; and his wife, Helena, sitting in the dust opposite him some twenty feet away.

Isaac ran forward and fell into his mother's embrace. A vinegar-dipped stone seemed to have lodged in Truman's throat, and his vision blurred with tears.

"Truman!"

Truman!

Dual warnings came to his ears and mind, and Truman looked around. Bullock hurried up from his left. Bad Hand looked on from his perpendicular view in the jar at the outlaw's feet. Truman turned to stare again at the black goo; the imp, he knew, in its weakened form. But this time there was no one he could rely on, no one he could defer to. Preacher Smith was dead, so, perhaps, was Shen Liu. And Makohlo-ka had returned to his tribe.

Truman sprang to his feet. He raced toward Helena. Her eyes widened, and she rose to meet him. Truman nearly knocked his wife down as he wrapped his arms around her in a fervent embrace. He kissed her lips, pouring as much love as he could into the action. Then, not daring to risk a moment more, he stooped and retrieved the empty bottle.

The perverse imp had crept, slug-like, into the shadow cast by the Franklin Hotel. Its survival sense told it that the darkness under the boardwalk would afford temporary safety and a place to hide while it healed and regained its strength.

Ignoring the pain from his bullet wound, Truman Bonner knelt and scooped the imp into his improvised glass prison. He shook the bottle until the obsidian glob plopped to the bottom, where it immediately began its slow but determined ascent.

Truman looked at his wife, trembling as the adrenaline left his body. "Did you happen to bring along a cork for this?"

Helena, now holding Isaac close, only tilted back her head and laughed.

Chapter 11
Tie a Knot in the Devil's Tail

"I still don't understand why we had to roll him over," Truman said.

"Because I refuse to shoot a man in the back," Sheriff Bullock said.

Truman didn't think the outlaw would have survived his burn injuries for long, but he said nothing more on the subject.

Hollister, they had decided, would be buried in a pine box; the imp needed something more substantial.

Three figures now stood two hundred feet inside the confines of a natural cavern near Deadwood.

"Isaac, set the bottle there on that ledge," Truman said. Isaac did as instructed and stepped back. "Now we dump the gunpowder we hauled in here and go back the way we came. Isaac, unravel this fuse and I'll light it at the mouth of the cavern. We'll bury this source of evil so deep that no one will ever find it."

"We should have enough gunpowder to bring down the whole damn mountain on it," Sheriff Bullock remarked.

Truman itched to be away from the bottled imp. "Then let's get to it."

* * *

The ground shook beneath their feet. Smoke and grit belched out of the cavern's entrance. The horses they'd ridden tossed their heads and pranced nervously. And then it was finished.

Truman and Helena embraced. Isaac stepped forward; his parents opened their arms to welcome him into the circle.

"We each faced death," Truman said.

Helena touched his bandaged shoulder and scarred face. "For that, I am sorry."

"But we helped each other, gave each other strength." Truman held both wife and son in a tight embrace. Part of him never wanted to let them go.

Helena's cheeks dimpled as she smiled. "Yes, and for that, I am thankful."

Despite the hell she'd been through, Truman still found her beautiful. "I acted like a damned fool, getting up on my high horse. Will you forgive me for that?"

Helena's eyes brimmed with tears. She nodded. "Of course. Will you forgive me?"

"Isaac and I need you to stay safe from now on. We need you to exercise … restraint."

Helena nodded. "I will do my best. I promise."

"That's all I can ask."

"There's too much wickedness and evil in this world," Helena observed. Isaac nodded his agreement.

"But there's a lot of goodness in it, too," Truman said.

"I feel like I've woken from a nightmare, but nightmares don't leave scars …" Tears finally spilled over her sunburned cheeks. Truman sensed there might be more that she wasn't yet ready to reveal.

He kept his fears in check and stroked her cheek. "We'll heal together."

"Why won't Isaac talk to me?" Helena's voice shook. "And what happened to his hair?" At this, she gave in to her guilt and sorrow. Sobs wracked her frame.

Truman held her close. "That's a story for another day. Just know that he still loves you with all his heart."

Helena quieted. She looked up at Truman, biting her lip. "Do you think that whatever got into Hollister will stay buried in the tunnel?"

Truman took a deep breath and held it. He gazed at his wife, and then at his son. He glanced at Sheriff Bullock standing near the horses. Bullock saw him looking and touched his fingers to the brim of his hat. On the ground at his feet, Bad Hand floated peacefully in his jar.

"If it comes back, we'll be ready," Truman said. "After what we've been through, I bet we could tie a knot in the tail of the Devil himself and kick his ass straight back to hell."

Helena grinned and grabbed the lapels of Truman's battered

oilskin duster. "I like the way you think, cowboy; from now on we work together." She planted a kiss on his lips.

"Together," Truman agreed. "Now let's go home."

* * *

The Bonners returned to their homestead on the edge of Sturgis.

They rested, healed, and tended to their chores. Helena wept bitter tears when she discovered the extent of her son's grievous injuries.

Sleepless nights reigned. Helena sipped burning liquid from a small flask she kept secreted away. Truman stayed up late brooding and reading from his weathered Bible. And Isaac, paralyzed by night terrors, often lay awake until the night sky turned gray.

Though they had vowed to work together, each chose to battle their demons alone.

They did their best, but sometimes one's best simply isn't enough. The road to hell is paved with good intentions, or so they say, and pride comes before a fall.

* * *

Summer gave way to fall. Winds tore leaves from branches, the grasses browned, and fall soon bolted away like a startled doe. Then winter swooped in and dropped blanket after blanket of snow across the region. With the arrival of spring, the snows melted and heavy rains followed, washing across the Black Hills and the nearby prairie. Atop a certain hill near Deadwood, something rode on those fast-running icy cold waters, traveling like poison in a bloodstream until it finally sprang free ...

GRAVE MARKER

S.L. Williams

The Dance

Chapter 1

Music. It's the only thing that makes this place bearable. I sit watching the drunken patrons in the tavern. Some are chasing girls, some drinking heavily. Hell, most are doing both. Not rich enough to live a life at court, we must make money the best way we can. Although, perversely, the very life we're barred from is the very life that feeds us money. They use us and make us feel like trash. They don't realize that if it wasn't for us, they would have to turn to their wives, who will not dance for them. But we will. We always dance.

Dancing is the only thing that keeps me sane as I glide through the tavern, fighting off advances and explaining gently that my soul isn't for hire. Well, at least not at the price they're offering. I love to dance. The way my skirt flows around my legs. The way my body moves in time with the music. Each sway and shimmy makes me feel so full of life. It makes my soul soar higher than the roof of this tavern. It's what makes me get up every morning and put on this corset and skirt. Dancing is what keeps me alive.

Chapter 2

I remember the first time I saw someone dance at a tavern. My mother had gone in to get my father out of the cups. I was supposed to stay outside, but it was cold. I didn't think it would hurt if I went inside just for a few moments, just long enough to get warm. There were so many men drinking, spending money, and lots of music. Then I saw five girls dressed in bright, bold colors on stage. As soon as they came onto the stage, the whole room became quiet, the lights dimmed, and for an eternity, the light was on them. They swerved and moved to each pulsing beat of the drums playing in the background. Their arms swirled above their heads gaily as they spun and skipped about. In my short life, it was the most amazing thing I had ever seen.

Secretly, I went back. I couldn't tell my mama where I was going. I just wanted to feel what the dancers must have felt when they were on stage. I couldn't wait to show my mama what I had learned. When I finished, I looked up into her eyes, and all of my excitement drained away from me. My mother just stared at me. She didn't move, and she didn't say anything. I finally ventured one word: "Mama." It was like I had opened a floodgate. Mama started beating me; she wouldn't stop slapping me. She said I would be a whore like the girls my papa ran off to every fortnight. I couldn't understand how something that gave me so much joy could cause so much pain for her. Thankfully, my father walked in, and he stopped Mama from hitting me. He made her explain why she was beating me. He scolded her, and then she turned on him, saying that it was his fault that I would grow into a Godless whore.

After that, things were strained between my parents. I did everything I could to make it up to Mama, but nothing I did would stop her from looking at me like I was something she scuffed off her shoe. One day Papa asked me to follow him to the market. I gratefully went; I loved Mama, but she made me feel so worthless it was a relief to get away for just a while. I remember walking aimlessly down the main road until we stopped outside of a large building. Papa smiled at me and told me he had a surprise for me. It was so unusual for him to pay any attention to me, let alone have surprises to show me.

We walked into the building, and it was so dark. My father told me to keep quiet and listen. I did as I was ordered, then I began to hear it. Softly, at first, but then it grew in volume. I could hear strings and the barest hint of a flute playing from somewhere. The music played, and a girl walked onto the stage. She stood there for just a moment, and I was treated to the second most breathtaking moment of my life. She started to dance. It wasn't like the girls in the tavern; it looked as if she was floating on her toes. Each spin and twirl seemed to levitate her into the air. Right then I knew that it was my destiny to be a dancer, and my father began to teach me how.

Chapter 3

Papa died; he left just enough for Mama to be comfortable, but not for much else. So I came to the tavern as soon as I was old enough, no longer being able to take the cold stares Mama had been giving me. In the beginning, I would dance every night. Pincher, the tavern's owner, would come from his storeroom with some new girl hanging off of his arm. He would slowly look around the room at his patrons and call out to me: "Blaze, dance for me!" I would stop whatever I was doing and move to the stage. I loved every minute, for this was the only time I stood out. The only time I outshone the sun, and I planned on living every minute of it.

But after all these years I see the truth of what I was ignoring. The patrons didn't watch me because they admired the way I moved. They just wanted me as some type of toy. Some living music box figure that would pirouette and move any way they pleased. I found that out the hard way. One nobleman had told Pincher that he wanted me to dance for him privately. Of course, Pincher prettied it up with nice words, and being full of myself, I believed every word he said about being admired, and the nobleman only wanting to watch me dance once more before he left the tavern the next day.

I had been so excited about my first private performance. I took extra care with my appearance. I walked up to the nobleman's room daydreaming about how he would be so impressed that he would take me away from this dingy little tavern. I was so wrapped up in my daydreams I failed to notice how strange it was that the nobleman was dressed in his nightshirt. I walked in, my dark red skirt and short black hair shining in the light from the oil lamps. I poured every ounce of my soul into my dance; my skin glistened in the light, my breathing was heavy, I thought my legs were going to give out on me. I curtsied after I finished and waited on the praise I was sure was to be mine.

The nobleman was just sitting there very still. I looked up, and the smile I saw on his face didn't make me feel very confident. I stood and began walking to the door, but the nobleman had the door locked from outside. He rose from his chair and came toward me. I backed away until there was nowhere else for me to go. He reached for me, and slowly my nightmares started. He wouldn't let me go. I begged and pleaded. He started touching me, and that was when I started to scream. I screamed and shouted till someone finally opened the door. The nobleman started swearing, and Pincher came in with an angry look on his face. He pushed me out of the room, telling me that he would talk to me tomorrow.

I went home that night crying and unable to catch my breath. The next morning was even worse. When I came in, Pincher started yelling and slapping me in front of the other girls. Some of them winced, while others were smiling. They always thought that I had been too proud and that I was only getting what I deserved. In a way, they had been right. I was stupid and so damned arrogant that I didn't read the signs. During my stay, I didn't remain innocent, but I did learn my lesson. I became a dancer exclusively; I wouldn't sell myself, and I used the fact that another tavern had offered me a job to make Pincher relent. It was a small victory, but a victory all the same.

Chapter 4

Tonight was one such evening of fighting off some rich man's offers. I went home before Pincher could try to wear me down into submitting; I was tired and in no mood to argue. I slipped out of my clothes and into my night shirts. Each movement was a silent agony as I curled into bed. I lay back onto my pillow and stared at the ceiling, my eyes filled with tears. I silently contemplated going to my mama and begging to come back. But I couldn't. I knew that if I went back she'd make me give up dancing. I couldn't do that. It would make the last five years of my life worth absolutely nothing. I turned onto my side and closed my eyes. If I didn't sleep, I'd look tired, and Pincher would make fun of me in front of the other girls. Slowly I drifted to sleep, the sound of cruel laughter echoing in my ears.

I woke up. Something in my room startled me, and I wasn't sure what it was. I just felt like I was not alone. I sat up in my bed and reached for the small dagger that I kept under the pillow. At first, I didn't see anything, but as my eyes adjusted to the light, I noticed a figure standing next to my window. I called for whoever it was to come out. The figure didn't move or make a sound for an endless minute. Then I heard soft laughter. Not like the drunken laughter from the tavern, but soft and clear, like water. The figure moved, and my eyes widened at the sight before me.

There was a man standing next to my window, but he had wings. As he moved closer to me, I could make out more details in the dim light. He was tall, and his hair was short and dark, like his eyes. The elegant and graceful lines of his body made me think he was a dancer, too. He was thin, but muscular; I could tell he never worked in any field. I was immediately frightened, but I couldn't look away; all I could do was grip my dagger tighter as he moved towards me.

He got to the foot of my bed. He looked down at me with a soft smile, and I finally moved my eyes to his wings. They were black, shiny black like the jewels some of the noble wives wore in their ears. My eyes widened once again, and I tried to make myself small against the back of my bed. He reached out to me, and I just stared at his hand. All of the dark prophecies about the devil coming to get me were spinning in my head. My mama was right. He was here, in front of me right now.

I continued looking at his hand, and I stammered before I could check myself: "Your wings are black." I winced, waiting for whatever punishment he intended to rain down upon me. I looked up once more, and I saw that his hand had settled at his side, but the smile had not left his face.

"Are you frightened?" he asked gently.

I nodded, stuttering, "You aren't an angel if your wings are black."

He stretched and continued to smile at me, shaking out his long dark wings. I fleetingly wondered if the feathers would fall to the floor, but that thought vanished as he moved closer to my end of the bed. He made a gesture as if asking if he could sit down. Not knowing what else to do, I nodded warily, my knife still clutched in my hand. Drawing my legs up to my chest so he couldn't touch me, I continued to watch him. He was beautiful, but he was obviously no messenger from heaven.

He gave me that smile again as he watched me nervously fiddle with my fingers, his teeth flashing in the lamplight. I saw that his canines came to small points at the end. My hands started to shake, and I knew that the dagger was useless. He watched my fingers carefully for a moment before laying his hand upon them. Energy flowed through me like a jolt of fire up my arm. It was if I had been dancing in front of a whole theater of people and I couldn't catch my breath. I looked up at him, and the grin became a small smirk. My face burned, and I could only thank the heavens that it was too dark for him to see. I moved my hand and pulled away from him once more.

"What do you want?" I asked, my voice barely above a whisper.

He chuckled and shook his head. He slid closer to me; his shoulders brushed mine as he made himself comfortable. "I don't want anything. I'm here for what you want," he said simply.

Millions of thoughts ran through my head: all of the things I wanted from the past week, the past two years, even some new thing I hadn't ever wanted before. My face burned again, and this time I was sure he could see it. The small smirk had not left his lips as he searched my eyes. I had been biting my lip to see if I was dreaming, and his eyes followed the movement.

"Whatever it may be," he added in a whisper.

I immediately stopped biting my lips, so as not to give him any ideas. I hadn't spent all of my time fending off nobles just to give in to the first handsome man I saw in my bedroom.

"What do you mean?" I asked. Anything to fill the silence. "I have no idea what I must do for this opportunity, but the price has to be high if it pays for anything I want."

"Whatever you ask for, you will receive," he said, moving nearer. "You will get one wish, one wish and one chance to have anything you desire."

He was so close to me, I knew he could feel my pulse through his hand. The sheer joy of having someone to be close to was not lost on me. I squirmed slightly as he wrapped his wings around me. I could feel his lips against my cheek and my eyes immediately closed.

He held me and described all of the things that I could have, all the things that I could do if I just made that one wish. He told me I could have anything I wanted, and I didn't have to do a thing for it. I immediately pulled away from him and got out of bed. I was not the brightest star in the sky, but I wasn't the dullest either. Nothing comes without a price. I'd learned that the hard way, and I wanted to know what his price was.

"Who are you?" I demanded. "What are you? How did you choose me?"

I waited for an answer, fleetingly remembering that I'd left the dagger on my bed. I cursed at myself silently. He looked surprised at my outburst, but smiled. He stretched out on my bed, propping his hand under his head and letting his gaze travel over me. I had never felt so open to anyone; it was as if his eyes gazed into my soul and memorized all they saw so that he could use it against me later.

"I am neither a devil nor an angel, but I have enough power to make your dreams come true. I grant wishes to those who deserve it. I give those who need it a chance to make their dreams come true, and ask nothing in return." He said all of this with a smile that was not as nice as it should have been with a statement that selfless.

"So you are here to grant the wish of someone you don't know? I don't even know your name." I was frightened, but I wanted to believe. He was cruel to offer this hope to me.

"My name is Souhait, and anything you ask for can be yours. Anything your heart desires is yours if you wish it." He leaned forward, tipping his chin so that his eyes were level with mine. "Don't you deserve it?"

I stared at him for a minute and laughed. I surprised myself at how harsh it sounded. I thought of everything I'd done since moving away. I remembered how my mother wept as I bid her goodbye. I thought of all the things I'd done to survive, and I wondered how on earth I could be deserving of such a gift.

"Why are you giving me this?" I asked, with a not-so-nice smile of my own. "There are lots of girls who deserve it far more than I do." I shook my head, trying to hold back the tears that threatened to pour down my cheeks. "I'm fine," I said. "I'm fine on my own. I don't need you."

Slowly, Souhait let his eyes fall from mine and looked around my quarters in the most insulting way. He took in the torn curtains and the cracked ceiling. He let his eyes rove over my sparse and obviously worn bedding. Finally, his eyes traveled over me, and they showed sad amusement. I frowned at him; I had never felt so invaded in my life.

"It's not as bad as it seems," I snapped. "I have a lot to be thankful for. I'm just waiting until it's my turn to dance on stage. I'll find a true gentleman who will ask me to dance for him, and then he'll take me to the theater and I'll become famous. I'll tour the world, dancing for rich and poor alike. There's nothing wrong with working at a tavern until my day comes." I hugged myself as I listened to what I was saying. I had been telling myself those lies for the past two years. I wanted to be a dancer, but every day my dream seemed farther and farther away.

Souhait watched me through my tirade, the same mocking amusement shading his eyes as he moved from the bed to stand next to me. He lifted my chin to look into my eyes before slowly pulling me back into his arms.

"Why do you delude yourself like that?" he asked. "You know that no true gentleman is going to find you in that tavern." His wings wrapped around me, and slowly he started rocking me back and forth. I relaxed into him, sharing his warmth. "Don't let this chance pass you by," he whispered. "With this one wish you can have — do — anything you want. With my help you'll dance for millions in places you've only dreamed of."

After a few moments Souhait turned me around, looked into my eyes, and placed a soft kiss upon my lips. My legs felt as if I had been dancing for hours. I would have agreed to anything, sold my soul if only to be near him, to be cared for always. I would give anything just so he would keep holding me like this. Just like this.

"What do you want?" he asked me. "Tell me what you would wish for if you did take me up on my offer. If you share your dreams with me, I promise that I will make them come true. I only want to help you to become who you are truly meant to be."

"I … I want to be a star dancer. I want to bring the dances of the tavern and the ballet of the stage together for everyone to see. I want to stop working at that tavern. I want to stop taking orders from people who don't value me, and who don't make me value myself." I couldn't stop myself. I poured out my soul to him. I screamed out every desire and craving I had ever held in my heart. I was breathing heavily and I couldn't stop the flood of words rushing out of my lips. "I wish to make my mother proud of me. I want to honor the man who showed me what dancing was."

"Is that all?" he asked, watching me with that small, secretive smile as I listed all of the things I would do.

"I want to make my name fly higher then stars. I'll open a dance school for girls who can't afford it." As I spoke, I became lightheaded. I felt his arms become lighter. He no longer felt real to my touch.

"Wait … Where are you going? Please don't go!" I called out to him, half begging, but he began to shift into a blinding light.

"Time is almost up, darling. If you want those things, take them. Say the words and they will be yours." He sounded as sad I felt that he was leaving. I sobbed miserably as his body turned into a light I couldn't hold.

I don't know what made me do it, but I embraced that light. I lay my head on what was left of his chest, and I whispered what he needed to hear. I yearn. I desire. I wish. *Je souhaite!* After that darkness, I remembered nothing.

Chapter 5

I woke up the next morning with a blinding headache. My limbs ached and my throat felt like it was made of sackcloth. I dragged myself out of bed slowly, looking around my room. Nothing had changed. I stretched and sighed sadly. It must have been a dream, something my mind invented to keep me warm. I held myself, trying to feel the warmth I felt last night. It was all just a dream after all: no warmth, no Souhait, and no wish. I looked out of my small window at the sunlit sky. It was almost time for work. I ran my hands through my hair and began to prepare. The whole time, I tried to keep my heart from breaking. Tears fell down my face as I moved about my room. It had been such a wonderful dream.

Chapter 6

The tavern was busy that evening. The lights shone brightly against the snow outside, and the music inside was deafening. I was so busy fetching drinks and slapping hands away from my thighs that I could barely think straight. I couldn't believe how many noblemen were there tonight. I rushed around like the rest of the barmaids, making sure everyone was comfortable and well fed. I just finished clearing a table when Pincher came out of his storeroom. His eyes fell on me. I watched him smile, and I knew what was coming. He gestured to the small stage at the head of the room and said two words.

"Blaze, dance."

The whole room went quiet as I climbed onto the stage; I looked to the minstrel. He smiled and began playing a soft tune about memories that one can't catch. At the first strains of music, my hands slipped above my head, and my hips slowly began rotating. As the song continued, I tried a few spins, and then tentatively lifted my leg in a sweeping motion above the stage. With each beat and pluck of the minstrel's hands, I became more daring. I pirouetted and leaped across the stage, blending the dances I did at work with the ballet I learned with my father. I knew without looking that everyone was watching me. They had forgotten their food, their drinks, and the women they had been so ardently chasing. Nothing else mattered to them or me but the way I moved across the stage. Towards the end, I wrapped my arms tightly around myself, remembering the demon who had visited my dreams. After all, I told myself, that's what he was. The music swelled, and I began to spin wildly. Each turn brought my hands higher along my body until they ended above my head. The song ended, and my heart raced wildly.

I waited for it. Then it started. First a few, and then many joined in. The roar of the applause became deafening. Even Pincher nodded approvingly before going back into his store room. I left the stage, and the euphoria I felt there didn't leave me for the rest of the night. I received lots of compliments and praise. I tried not to let it affect me, but I couldn't let it go. I knew that dancing should always feel like this.

Chapter 7

My pockets practically jingled as I moved through the room. Thoughts of the new blanket I could buy made me feel dreamy and content. I finished washing off the last of my tables, and I prepared to leave for the evening. Just as I pulled on my shawl, Pincher called me to his store room. I felt apprehensive, but went anyway. I could always say no to whatever it was he wanted. It was probably some persistent noble trying to secure my favors for the night.

I sighed heavily as I walked into the room. Sure enough, Pincher was not alone. A tall, handsome man with long white hair was sitting on the opposite side of the table. Pincher motioned for me to come and stand beside him so that the noble could see me better. I tried to hold back an irritated sigh and turned around to leave. I'd had this conversation one time too many, and I refused to do anything that would get rid of the wonderful feeling I had.

"I'm sorry, but I do not do that sort of thing. I'm sure one of the other dancers will gladly service you." I didn't even get to take my first step before I felt a hand clasping mine. I looked at the noble coldly.

Didn't he understand that I said no?

I tried to pull away again. The noble drew me back into the room. Pincher, smiling, got up from his chair and walked out of the door, giving me a cold smile before closing it. I glared at the door as I heard the soft click of the lock from outside, and I turned around to see the noble watching me steadily. I tensed, waiting for him to pounce, but the noble walked over to where Pincher had been sitting and motioned me to the chair opposite him.

"Please, sit down," he said. He looked at me imploringly. "If you don't like what I have to say, I will let you go. I have the key; I will not try to deter you from going, if that is what you wish once you hear me speak."

I shrugged and sat down. If it would make that door open a little faster, I would play his games. I needed a good story to fall asleep to that night, anyway. I watched him watching me. I saw how young he was, and it took me by surprise; the way he carried himself made him seem older. He began by telling me how lovely my dance was. I placed my hands over my lips, trying to hide a sneer. That's how they all started. "You danced so well. I had to be near you. Let me twirl with you in my arms as you did on the floor. Let me hold you, and let the nightmares go away just a little while." Nothing but empty promises and bigger lies, and I didn't want to hear any of it.

"My father is the Maestro of the local theater, and I would like you to audition this full moon's eve for the next concert. Your dance was beautiful, and I have never seen anything like it before. I know that my father will love it as I do. My name is Espoir from the house of Desir.

I would be honored if I could call at your home to escort you to the audition." His words were rushed, but I heard no deceit.

I had dreamed of this so many nights. Yearned and begged with all of my heart for some noble to rescue me from this place. But when Espoir mentioned calling on me at my home, I shook my head vigorously. It would not do for him to see my home. He would take one look at that hovel and run away laughing into the night.

"I'm sorry, I don't know you very well, so I would rather meet you there." I brazened out the half-lie. I would rather die than allow him to see my home.

"I understand that you want to be cautious, but it's better if I pick you up at your home. I can make sure you get there safely in my carriage," he said, the beginning of a frown on his lips.

"It's truly not necessary, but if you want to make sure I get there safely, why don't I just meet you here?" I suggested this as an alternative to mollify him. No sense in making him angry when he gave me my chance.

It was happening; it was what I'd always dreamed of! He unlocked the door, making me promise once more that I wouldn't stand him up. I promised vehemently, and I walked out into the night. My whole soul was warm from this new surprise. I sighed happily as I thought of going to the market tomorrow. I would need something to audition in. I could only smile as I crawled into bed. Even if I didn't make it, I could die knowing that I at least had the chance to become a star.

Chapter 8

The next two days passed by in a blur as if I hadn't been living them, but saw them in a dream. I danced all night at the tavern, half for money and half for practice. I made sure that not one of my steps was misplaced. I poured my heart into each performance, lapping up every ounce of applause and praise that I could get. I had to; it might be gone tomorrow, and I wanted these memories to last. The night of the audition was here, and Espoir was waiting for me beside his coach.

It was so grand. Blue with gold trim, pulled by four black horses. I felt like a queen sitting on the cushioned seats, watching the world fly past as the horses galloped through the streets. I could only smile as Espoir made small talk. My mind was fixed on the audition and whether I would be able to compete with the other dancers. I felt Espoir's eyes upon me as we made our way to the theater. I looked back at him steadily and just let the first words that came to mind fall bluntly from my lips.

"I'm not going to sleep with you for this."

I wanted to slap myself. I just knew the coach was going to stop and he was going to throw me out, but Espoir just laughed and ran his hands through his loose white hair.

"I don't put much stock in my looks," he said, "but I'm sure I don't have to trick women into sleeping with me."

"I'm sorry," I said, regretting my sharp words. Here he was only trying to help me and I was throwing his kindness back in his face. "Thank you for this chance. I hope I won't embarrass you in front of your father."

He just nodded with a smile and continued making small talk as we made our way to the theater.

We reached the theater, and he led me to a room where all the other dancers were waiting their turn. As soon as I walked in, I felt like a wren among so many perfect swans. Their hair was tied in neat buns, and their dresses were so light and delicate. I moved to an open section of the bar and begin a short exercise that would warm me up. I was halfway through when I felt someone tap me on the shoulder. I turned and looked at the girl with a smile.

"Who did you sleep with to get in here?" she asked, causing my smile to falter.

The whole room went quiet, and I just gaped at her. I didn't know what to say. I had been around girls who didn't like me before, but she didn't even know me. The other girls were waiting on my answer. They obviously thought the same thing she did.

"I didn't sleep with anyone," I said. "I'm just a dancer like you."

She laughed. "You're common," she said. "There is no way you are anything like me." The other girls tittered, and I could feel my face burn. I was sure that once I was around other dancers like my-self, they would recognize me as one of their own.

"I didn't sleep with anyone," I repeated. "And I have just as much right to be here as you do." I was so angry that tears started welling in my eyes, and I barely got control of myself when the director asked us to follow him to the stage. Everyone started moving to the door, some of the girls shouldering me out of the way. I sighed, taking slow, calming breaths. I had to perform. It was just like the tavern; I had to block it out or I wouldn't do my best; but heavens, it hurt!

Each girl got her chance on stage, the first girl being the one who had been rude to me. Her name was Despiar. In truth, she was a fine dancer, light and willowy, like a feather. She glided across the stage to some obscure floating piano piece she said had been written for her. The other girls clapped as she walked off stage. I didn't miss the cold smile she gave me as she went by, nor did I miss the cold looks coming from some of the other girls. I stiffened and ignored them. I couldn't let them see how much each look was like a knife through my soul. I waited through each audition, noting who was fair, and who was ex-cellent. I watched each dancer until it was my turn.

Every girl had been required to bring a sheet of music with her. I didn't have much to choose from, only having the music my father made me learn before he died, so I had picked one of the faster-paced pieces. I gave the music to the conductor and curtsied to the Maestro, wincing when he exclaimed loudly about how his son should keep his harlots where they belonged. That brought a trill of laughter from the girls in back, but I ignored it and looked up at Espoir. He stared back at me with eyes of the clearest green and nodded for me to start. I motioned for the conductor to begin and cleared my head; I couldn't let the anger cloud my audition.

But I couldn't stop it. The anger just welled up inside of me as the music began. I couldn't help myself. As the first few beats of music began, I looked up into the eyes of the Maestro. I let every inch of anger and hate I felt at being treated that way pour into my dance. Every whirl and eddy of movement reflected how I felt about the people who laughed at me. As the music became faster, I let my hips rotate and swivel to each staccato note. I couldn't hold myself back any longer. I glided and flitted through the air, each movement short and economical. I didn't even feel tired as my hands touched the floor and I brought myself up once again. I didn't hear the gasps and the surprise because I didn't care. I didn't want any of their praise. I just wanted them to see what I could do and how dangerous it was to cross me. I wanted them to feel the power that I felt as the song continued to play. Towards the end, I slowly stopped spinning and stretched onto the floor, laying there until I was ready to move again.

When I was done, there was no clapping, there was no applause. I didn't expect any; I didn't want any. I just wanted to leave that room before they all saw me cry. I ran from the hall, hearing Espoir's voice faintly calling me back. I ran until I found a quiet room and wept. It had been nothing like I thought it was going to be. It was just one more childish fantasy that shattered in my face. I cried until I could find no more tears. Then I decided to find Espoir. He had given me the chance I dreamed of. Even if it didn't go as planned, I needed to thank him.

I left the room and started walking down the hall. I stopped when I heard a faint giggling. I watched as the door opened, and Despiar walked out, pulling up the sleeve of her dancing costume. She stopped when she saw me, going as still as a statue. She was about to come towards me when the Maestro walked out behind her, pulling his pants on. He stopped when he saw me. I just stood there, not knowing what to do. I felt a laugh bubbling up in my throat. Noble girls were the same as common girls; they just had more money to make them comfortable while they did what they had to do to survive. Using someone else's money was far different from having your own.

"What was that you said about leaving your harlots at home, father?" Espoir asked his father with a smirk as he walked up behind me.

Despiar gasped angrily and turned on her heel and stalked off, her head high. I looked back into the Maestro's clear blue eyes, and he looked into my dark ones, and I know he saw the amused anger in them.

"Son, would you follow me into the study?" The Maestro pulled himself together and turned to me. "Would you be so kind as to go wait with the other girls?"

I walked back to the practice hall and saw Despiar sitting in the middle of a group of girls who tittered when I walked in; they wouldn't meet my eyes. I knew that she had gotten what she wanted. I could only hope that it was worth it. The Maestro came into the hall. Despiar was given the lead, and I got a supporting role that made some of the girls gasp. Espoir shrugged apologetically and I gave him a small smile.

It was not his fault. The Maestro wouldn't look at me as he laid out the rehearsal times and what we needed to bring to each practice. I didn't know where I was going to get most of the supplies, but I knew I would work hard to get them.

Espoir took it upon himself to take me home. I told him that it was unnecessary and that he could just drop me off at the tavern. He sighed, and I could hear the sadness in it as he directed the coachmen to take me back to the tavern.

"Thank you," I told him politely as I got out of the carriage, stopping once he took my hand. "I mean it; thank you for taking me to the audition. I will never forget your kindness."

"If you tell me where you live I can pick you up for practice." He smiled, and a small trill of fear raced up my back.

"No, really, it's fine. I'll be working anyway, so it's easier just for you to meet me here," I stammered, knowing I would do anything to keep him from seeing my home. He frowned, but did not argue further, for which I was thankful.

I watched as the coach carried Espoir away. Then I twirled and danced down the street to my home. I walked into my room and it felt like a palace. I looked towards my window, hoping to see the demon who made my wish come true. True, I hadn't become a star, but I was on my way, and it felt so wonderful. I wanted to thank him, beg him to hold me once more.

I looked about and waited. I wrapped my arms about myself in a hug, and my heart felt empty. I saw nothing, and I started to get ready for bed. As I looked to the window once more, I resigned myself to the fact that he wasn't coming back. I sat on my bed, looking at the full moon. Sending a silent prayer to whoever would listen, thanking them for giving me my chance.

Chapter 9

The coming weeks passed in a long haze. My schedule consisted of practice and work. I was tired, but I didn't care. I practiced in the theater, then on the stage of the tavern, drawing customers with what Pincher called "a pinch of class." Espoir picked me up from the tavern in the morning and dropped me off in the evening. Sometimes, he stayed and had dinner with me; other times he took me to breakfast before practice. It was like I had found the friend that I'd always been looking for. He watched me closely sometimes, but I didn't mind it anymore. It was just his way.

The night of the performance arrived. I was so nervous. Pincher would be in the audience, and he made sure to brag about it to everyone who would listen; how he found me and polished me up so that the world would see me shine. I ignored that. My thanks were only for two people; Souhait and Espoir.

Everyone danced marvelously. The show went smoothly and the applause was deafening. When the curtain call came, Despiar proudly accepted the roses that came from being the prima ballerina. Each part came out in level of importance. I was fourth in line. I just knew that the crowd would be clapped out. I was wrong. I couldn't leave the stage for the applause that echoed through the hall. There were so many roses and cheers of bravo. I couldn't stop myself from grinning at the joy all these people felt because of the show.

At the after-party, many congratulated the Maestro and Despiar. The champagne flowed, and there were so many wealthy nobles there. I felt as if I was a fish in the wrong pond. I tried to stay to the side as much as I could, but Espoir found me and dragged me to the center of the room.

"Where have you been hiding? Everyone wants to meet you," he asked when we got there.

"I was by the fireplace," I stammered, and I could feel my face burning brightly. I didn't want to explain that I wanted to stay as warm as I could before I went home. Tomorrow I would definitely buy that blanket.

Espoir introduced me to many of the nobles. Some I had met at the tavern, others I had never seen before. Their congratulations were genuine, if a bit stilted. What did you say to someone who had seen you at your worst, and whom you didn't expect to see in your circles? Espoir reached the Maestro, who was standing next to Despiar. She didn't look happy to see me.

"She's angry that you upstaged her," Espoir whispered to me.

I didn't think that was true. Although I didn't like her, I knew she danced wonderfully. But as I looked into her eyes, I saw that he was partially right. The look she gave me was so cold I wanted to be in my drafty little room again.

"Congratulations." Despiar's words were as frosty as her gaze.

"Same to you." My reply was just as stilted. No need to pretend we were friends, after all.

"You were wonderful! The next time I have a composition, I hope to you see you audition for it." The Maestro also praised me. Apparently money made him forget where I came from.

Despiar glared at me; I nodded and took a step back from her. I just looked at her, and I hoped that look conveyed the message that I wanted to scream: *Look who you slept with to get your part!*

Finally, the party came to an end. I was half asleep when we arrived at the tavern. I stumbled down from the carriage, giving Espoir a friendly kiss on the cheek. I stood there as always, waving to the coach as it galloped down the street. When it was out of sight, I made my way home. I slipped out of my clothes and got into my bed, shivering but happy as I started to drift off to sleep.

I didn't have my head on the pillow for a moment before my door opened. I gasped as I saw Espoir looking around my small room, taking in every detail of the shabby apartment. I looked down and would not meet his eyes, even when he called my name.

"Blaze, why did you not tell me where you lived?" he asked. "It's closer to the theater then the tavern is."

"I didn't want you to be ashamed of where I lived. I thought that if you knew exactly what I was, you wouldn't want to be my friend any longer," I explained, looking away once more.

Espoir looked at me for a moment before he hugged me. I sat

there in shock, not sure of what to say or do. I couldn't hide any-more, and I couldn't pretend that this didn't happen. Espoir leaned back to look at me, and his smile was small and shy.

"It doesn't matter, Blaze. I've known where you lived all along." My gaze lifted to meet his and he just smiled and shrugged. "It isn't safe for a lady to be walking the streets at night alone."

I just sat there, fiddling with my fingers, not sure of what to say. He lifted my chin and placed a soft kiss on my lips. I pulled back and looked at him in wonder for a minute before leaning back to return the kiss — tentatively at first, but the kiss soon grew more demanding.

Chapter 10

The next morning, I woke up and I found that I was not cold at all. I was quite warm and very comfortable. I couldn't figure it out until Espoir tightened his arms around my waist. My eyes grew wide, and I turned to look at Espoir, smiling sleepily.

"I should go," he said with a smile as his finger drew across my lips. "Father wanted to discuss something with me this morning and I dare not be late."

I nodded numbly. I couldn't believe what I had done. I would never see him again and this was his brush off. I placed a soft kiss on his lips and nodded bravely once again. All good things came to an end; I guessed this was my ending.

Espoir watched me as I moved from the bed, raking my fingers through my short hair. I told him he could clean up near the stove. I looked outside and saw that it was almost time for me to go to work. At least that was something I could do to keep my mind off of my stupidity. I silently berated myself as I pulled my clothes on. How could I be so dumb? I had my chance right in front of me, and I wasted it on one night of warmth. In the midst of my anger at myself, I felt warm arms wrap around my waist. I look up over my shoulder, and I saw Espoir smiling at me. He had gotten dressed as well and was coming over to say goodbye.

"I honestly don't know what to say." Stammering, I smiled and shrugged helplessly.

"You didn't enjoy yourself?" Espoir looked a bit worried. He sighed when I didn't answer right away and began to speak angrily to himself. "I knew I should have been more careful. I didn't want to do anything to hurt you, but I love you so much I wasn't thinking. I'm so sorry, Blaze."

I looked at him blankly for a moment, trying to figure out what I had missed. He cupped my cheek in his hands and tilted my face up to his. I searched his face trying to find answers to my unasked questions before telling him the truth. "I love being with you, Espoir. I would never have wanted to be anywhere else."

He gave me a bright smile and hugged me close. I could do nothing but return the hug and breathe in his scent. So comforting, like that blanket I had been dreaming about buying.

Espoir let me go. "I have to go. I want to see you again tonight so that we can talk. I'll meet you at work, don't go anywhere without me."

He left, but not before stealing a few more kisses and making me promise not to go anywhere until I saw him. I sat on my bed for a moment before jumping and hugging myself close. I couldn't remember ever being so happy. I quickly finished getting dressed and headed to the market. I had to get that blanket before work.

I slipped through the market in a happy daze. I actually had money for once, so it made looking at all of the things I wanted even more special. I finally found the woman who sold the blankets. She was short and crafty looking with shifty eyes. She watched me look through the blankets for a moment before motioning me over behind the counter. She pulled out a large blanket made of dark red satin. She took my hand and slipped it across the fabric.

"This one is special, my dear. It will keep you warm on long winter nights, and protect you from evil." The old women smiled at me with her broken teeth, and I couldn't help but notice how sharp they are. I bought the blanket from her, mainly because I wanted to get away. I hated the color; it looked like blood. I remembered the old women's smile and I shuddered inwardly.

I didn't think of it again until after work that night. Nobles were coming from all over to watch me dance since they saw me in the ballet. They congratulated me and offered me money for various favors, but I turned them down politely, thinking of my meeting with Espoir. I laughed and danced the whole night until I saw Espoir coming through the door. He smiled at various friends and shook his head at various advances. He finally reached me, and I wrapped my arms around him tightly.

He returned the hug and led me out into the cool night air. I told him to stop a moment, and I went and retrieved my blanket. I laughed and showed it to him, telling him about the woman who sold it to me. He laughed tightly and gave the blanket an uneasy look before continuing to lead me outside to his carriage. We both got in, and he sat on the opposite side of me. That was strange; he always sat next to me. I shrugged it off. The blanket was a bit large, and he probably thought it would be more comfortable to sit on the other side. It didn't matter; I loved looking into his eyes.

We made small talk until we reached his home. I stepped out of the carriage with the blanket wrapped around me, and Espoir walked me in. I wasn't sure what was going on; he seemed distant. I chewed my lip quietly, hoping I hadn't offended him in some way. We reached his room, and I closed the door behind me. I dropped the blanket onto the floor and threw myself into his arms.

"I don't know what I did to insult you, but I'm sorry," I stammered and babbled apologies for what seemed like forever.

He just smiled at me and wrapped his arms around my waist and tightly placed soft kisses along my jawline. I sighed and leaned into each kiss. It was so warm in his arms. I couldn't stop him from slipping the straps of my dress to my shoulders; I didn't even want to stop him. I just wanted to lose myself in this feeling. He quickly undressed me and for endless moments we made love.

I lost all sense of time, and I didn't know what hour it was when I slowly tiptoed off of the bed. There was a fireplace in his bedroom that looked so inviting. I picked up my blanket from the floor near the door and wrapped it about myself. I moved to an overstuffed white chair and snuggled into it. I drowsily stared into the fire, watching the flames dance and jump from the wood, like small dancers to their own tune. I was almost asleep when I heard something whisper, "Leave now! Get out of that room while you can!"

I looked around, trying to figure out where the voices were coming from.

"Stop it," I hissed to Espoir. "It's not funny, and it's scaring me."

The whispers just became more insistent.

I grabbed my clothes from the floor and slipped them on. I wrapped the blanket around my shoulders tighter and quietly slipped out of the room, making my way down the stairs as the voices continued to urge me out of the house. I walked towards the door and stopped. I berated myself for being silly and began to head back the way I came. I looked into the living room with the large grand fireplace.

The flames in the fireplace began to take the shape of my angel. I stepped back, and my lips parted in a scream that never came. I tried to go back upstairs to warn Espoir, but a row of flames blocked my path. Souhait leaped from the fire and shook his head, angrily pointing to the door. I nodded slightly and ran from the house into the cold night.

Chapter 11

I woke up the next morning to men lightly slapping my face trying to wake me. I looked towards the house and saw that it was a charred mess.

"Espoir! Where is he? Where is Espoir?" I screamed.

They shook their heads sadly and pointed to the wreckage of the house.

I screamed. I screamed, and I couldn't stop. I couldn't stop the ice sliding through my veins, and I couldn't stop the way my body began shaking. Espoir's father came over and held me.

"Leave her with me. Don't worry, dear. I'm sure it was quick. You were lucky to get out. You were knocked out by a beam on your way to get help." The workers left, and I cried in his arms until there was nothing left.

"That is a complete lie," I sobbed. "There was a demon there. He burned the house down. I saw him!"

"You're just in shock my dear. Come with me." He chuckled sadly and ushered me away from the wreckage.

Desir took me back to his home and gave me warm tea. I cried into my blanket, not sure of what to say. I watched him run his hands through his gray hair and look over at me. Eventually he walked over to his desk, and pulled out a parchment sheet filled with music.

"Espoir wrote it for you." He let me look it over for a few moments before asking, "Will you perform it in his honor?"

I nodded vigorously. I would do this. I would dance for him one last time. I couldn't help but hear the old man's soft sobs over his beloved son.

Each week of practice was long and hard. Espoir's dance was quite demanding. I almost collapsed into exhaustion trying to complete the complicated steps. Each movement and step had to be right or I would not go on. I began to lose sleep, and I stopped eating. By the time the show was ready, I had at least five costume refittings. The seamstress told me that I was beautiful. I laugh harshly and shook my head. No, I was never beautiful. How could beauty come from such selfishness? I would make sure that the dance was perfect.

The seats were packed with nobles and their wives. Some even brought their mistresses to see Espoir's first and last work. It was so sad watching Espoir's father tell the audience about the piece; how he wrote it when he fell in love with me, and how he would always be remembered. I couldn't stop myself from crying when he told the audience about Espoir's life. Espoir's father finished the speech and left the stage. He motioned for the Maestro to start playing and the curtains rose, revealing the rest of the cast and me.

The music began fast, making all of the dancers jump and flit about. Each drumbeat made the floor jump and pulse with its rhythm as we raced across the stage. I slowly allowed myself to lose all my senses to the music, and my body took over. I danced and swerved, letting my hips rise and fall to each exotic beat. Espoir had combined the best of both worlds into one ballet: the hot steamy world of the bar, melding with the light open air of the ballet. He had done what I had been trying to do for years. I couldn't help but cry as the performance continued. I never wanted it to end. Each step, each gesture brought Espoir back to me.

The dance ended and the roar was deafening. There was not one person sitting down. I took my bows with Espoir's father. The clapping became louder as he placed a soft kiss on my hand.

I went home at the end of the show. I had been asked to stay, but I took my blanket and headed home. I didn't even feel the cold as I walked to my part of town.

I entered my apartments numbly. The applause still rang in my ears as I sat on my bed. I looked to the window, and as I expected, Souhait was standing there waiting for me. I watched him for a time, not sure of what to say. He watched me with his soft, slightly mocking smile.

"Why?" I whispered.

He laughed and moved closer to me with a wide grin. I noticed how sharp his fangs were and I shuddered inwardly. "I did you a favor. Espoir was going to ask you to marry him, and that would have stopped your career as a dancer. I promised you that I would make you a star, and that means removing obstacles. After all, if you had been married, you would have been happy and content with that life and not have moved on."

"Plus, I was a tad jealous." He chuckled, and I just watched him, still feeling the numbness from the last few days. I looked into his beautiful face and began to cry.

"Bring Espoir back. He didn't deserve this! He was going to be someone. I cannot keep a gift that robs someone else of theirs," I screamed and moved from the bed to beat my hands angrily across his chest.

He just grabbed my hands and smiled. He turned me around and pulled me roughly against his chest. He slowly rocked me, and this time I found no comfort in it. I felt him grin against my neck, and I remembered the old woman's smile the day I bought my blanket. I shuddered. He held me for what seemed like forever.

"What do you want?" I asked.

Souhait grinned again. This time I felt the pure evil in it as he looked me over. He let his hands slide over my cheeks and my shoulders. I cringed, which made his smile wider.

"I'll let you have another wish, but this one comes with a price," he said.

"What is the price?" I asked with resignation. I hated his smile.

"You just have to do whatever I want, for as long as I want."

I just nodded numbly to his request. "You have to bring Espoir back alive and well. I want the chance to say goodbye when you do."

"Whatever you wish." Souhait smiled his infuriating smile and nodded. He turned me around slowly and pointed to the bed.

I looked to where his hands gestured, and there was Espoir sleeping peacefully on my bed. I ran to him I let my hands run over his face and arms, confirming that he was real. Espoir woke up and smiled into my eyes sleepily.

"What's wrong, and why are you crying?" he asked, and I shook my head. We didn't have time.

"I'm leaving, Espoir," I told him quietly.

He sat up and shook his head angrily. "Don't go, Blaze. I love you, and I want to marry you. I have a play that I wrote just for you."

I laid my hands on his lips to stop the flow of words and tried to explain the best way I could. "I made a promise to an angel that if he brought you back, I would go with him."

Espoir shook his head and pulled me to him. I felt so warm, just like that first night, and I didn't want to let go. I knew that I must, though, and I slowly rose from the bed. Souhait waited for me by the window, and Espoir got up from the bed. He stepped between me and the demon.

"Blaze, you don't belong to anyone. You can't leave me."

I smiled sadly and moved in front of him. I wasn't sure what Souhait would do if I defied him, and I didn't want to find out. I placed a soft kiss on Espoir's lips. "I love you so much, Espoir. I hope you are happy."

Souhait waved his hands, and the dark red blanket flew to him. It began to shine and shift form until it became a pair of soft, dark red ballerina shoes. He handed them to me with a mocking grin, and I couldn't help but hate him. I pulled away from Espoir and moved to a chair. I slipped the shoes on, and they began to glow and mold to my feet.

"Those shoes are your bonds. They will stay on your feet until I die or the bonds are somehow broken," Souhait explained as I stood in them. "If you try to take them off, they will squeeze your feet until you learn to behave yourself." I nodded and shuddered, that familiar cold feeling creeping in.

I looked lifelessly into Espoir's eyes, then looked away. I couldn't stand the look of helplessness that I saw there. I knew it had to be mirrored in my eyes. Souhait held his hand out to me and I took it reluctantly.

"Goodbye," I whispered to Espoir once more.

Souhait moved behind me and took me to the window. One moment I was avoiding Espoir's eyes and the next I saw stars as Souhait whisked me away into the night, leaving Espoir screaming after us.

"You will be my personal ballerina. Every night you will perform and I will be your personal audience. Don't cry, my love. After to-night, they will speak of your story forever, and you'll be famous." I couldn't keep the tears from flowing as Souhait's last words drifted across my ears. "Just the way you wanted."

ABOUT THE AUTHORS

Dominic Stabile is a writer of weird fiction. His stories have appeared in numerous magazines, including *Sanitarium Magazine*, *The Horror Zine*, *Atticus Review*, *Fossil Lake III: Unicornado!*, and *Cyclopean #1*. His first book, a Punk Noir Bizarro Thriller entitled, *Stone Work*, was released by *Mirror Matter Press* in 2016. A follow-up novel, *Death Central*, is set to be released in 2017. He has held jobs as a warehouse worker, cashier, bookstore associate, textbook manager, and carpenter. When not writing, reading, or hitting things with a hammer, he enjoys watching movies, relaxing with his girlfriend, and bourbon.

Adrian Ludens is the author of two collections*: Bedtime Stories for Carrion Beetles* and *When Bedbugs Bite*. Recent and upcoming publication appearances include: *Cranial Leakage: Tales from the Grinning Skull, Vol. II* (Grinning Skull Press), *D.O.A. III* (Blood Bound Books), *The Fourth Book of Spectral Horror Stories* (Tickety Boo Press), *Dark Horizons* (Elder Signs Press), and *Let Them In 2* (Time Alone Press). Adrian is a fan of hockey, many genres of music, and exploring abandoned buildings. He is an Active member of the Horror Writers Association. For a cover gallery, links to free stories, news and more, visit www.adrianludens.com.

S.L. Williams spends a lot of time thinking about the lives of people who don't exist. She has worked her way through college on the whims of the angels and demons that live in her head. Thankfully their residence allows her to share their stories with others. She is very thankful for her family, since they put up with her feverish writing binges. She is also grateful to those that take the time to walk through the darkness with her. Her work has been seen in *Zombie Guide Magazine*, NrdFeed.com, *Gothic Fairy Tales for Melancholy Children*, Castle Publishing, and History and Mystery LLC.

Press
Presents

Grave Markers, Volume 2
(includes Hal Bodner's *Tolerance*, Sebastian Bendix's *Shriek of the Harpy*, and Russell Coy's *The One Who Lies Next to You*)

NOTE: Grave Markers are available individually in digital format or as a 3-in-1 print compilation.

Grave Markers, Volume 1
(includes Richard Black's *Nikolis Cole: the Low-Rise Saint*, Sebastian Bendix's *Rock, Paper, Scissors*, and Joshua Rex's *Coattails*)

www.ingramcontent.com/pod-product-compliance
Lightning Source LLC
Chambersburg PA
CBHW051239170626
46809CB00004B/1396